THE MIDNIGHT TEST

RITE WORLD: LIGHTGROVE WITCHES
BOOK 1

JULIANA HAYGERT

COPYRIGHT

AUTHOR'S NOTE

I hope you enjoy reading *The Midnight Test*!

Don't forget to sign up for my Newsletter to find out about new releases, cover reveals, giveaways, and more!

If you want to see exclusive teasers, help me decide on covers, read excerpts, talk about books, etc, join my reader group on Facebook: Juliana's Club!

RITE WORLD

Welcome to the RITE WORLD!

Free Novella:
The Vampire Hunt

Novellas:
The Hunter Path
The Light Calling
The Light Witch

Rite World:
The Vampire Heir (Book 1)
The Witch Queen (Book 2)
The Immortal Vow (Book 3)
The Warlock Lord (Book 4)
The Wolf Consort (Book 5)
The Crystal Rose (Book 6)
The Wolf Forsaken (Book 7)

The Fae Bound (Book 8)
The Blood Pact (Book 9)

Rite World: Blackthorn Hunters Academy
The Demons Kiss (Book 1)
The Hunter Secret (Book 2)
The Soul Bond (Book 3)
The Shadow Trials (Book 4)
The Immortal Vow (Book 5)

Rite World: Lightgrove Witches
The Midnight Test (Book 1)
The Midnight Spell (Book 2)
The Midnight Flame (Book 3)
The Midnight Secret (Book 4)

And more to come!

runs into a very arrogant vampire. Her first instinct is to kill him, after all, he's a supernatural and demon hunters are taught to end all evil.

Cain is a vampire prince. Because of his status, he's in charge of making sure humans don't find out about his kind. During a routine investigation, he bumps into a very sexy demon hunter and he wonders what she's doing on his way.

However, the case grows much bigger for Norah and Cain to handle alone. To find the truth and win this battle, the vampire and the demon hunter will have to hunt together —without killing each other.

How well could this end?

THE MIDNIGHT TEST

An unprepared witch. A mysterious human. And a quest that will test them both …

Hazel always knew she was one of the weakest witches of her generation. For a moment there, she even cared about that status.

Not anymore. She's determined to live her life as a normal human—with exception for the occasional ghost hunting. What can she do if the damn spirits won't leave her alone?

But when she finally settles into a new routine, Hazel receives a message that changes everything: the Lightgrove Coven, one of the most powerful witch covens in the world, grants her a rare chance to join them, but only if she passes a dangerous test on Friday the Thirteenth.

At first, Hazel wants to disregard the message. But who is she kidding? This is an opportunity she can't say no to.

Everything is going unexpectedly fine until a human steps in Hazel's way. Sean is mysterious, hot, and inexplicably alluring. Despite Hazel's best attempts to ignore him, she can't. And when Sean's fate entwines with Hazel's task, it puts everything at risk—not just her test, but also their own lives.

1

THE FORCE LIKE A COLD WIND MIXED WITH AN ELECTRIC pulse ripped through me, and I gasped. What the ...? Dozens of bad words crossed my mind, and I would have spat them if my cell phone hadn't dinged.

So, did it work?

I sighed. If whatever was haunting this place stopped playing, maybe I could start the ritual and find out.

Hang on.

I knelt on the floor and resumed drawing a summoning circle. I could feel the entity nearby, as if it were watching me, wondering what I was doing. I looked up, searching for the moon, but both four-story dorm buildings did a great job of hiding it from me.

It was almost two in the morning, and even though it

was Sunday, most students seemed to have turned in early. Probably because fall classes officially started tomorrow. Good thing too, because I didn't need any curious eyes.

I finished the circle and withdrew a small leather pouch from inside my tote, which was lying on the ground near my feet. I opened the pouch and shook the contents into the palm of my left hand. The red hawthorn berry powder was running low, but I should have enough for tonight's ritual. I made a mental note to stop by the Midnight Cauldron to buy more.

Focusing on my task, I pinched the red powder with my fingers and sprinkled the dust on the ground, forming a six-pointed star in the center of the circle. After making sure there were no gaps in the star, I cinched the pouch and threw it back in my tote. I pulled out my phone and sent a message to my sister Amanda.

Done.

Now place the crystals on each point of the star and step into the circle, and then call it.

I rolled my eyes.

I know.

Sorry. Force of habit.

Her powers manifested when she was eight, and she started learning magic right away. I was six then, and even though I still hadn't manifested, I sat through her lessons. I absorbed everything. Amanda's affinity appeared when she was thirteen—the ability to turn water into ice, but only in small quantities. It was a fairly simple affinity, but she was happy with it. Until then, I hadn't even made a single spark with my fingers. My mother thought all the time I had spent studying had been a waste.

Finally, on my sixteenth birthday, a sliver of magic appeared. To my mother's disgrace, I had been the oldest witch we knew to receive my magic, and also the weakest. However, I knew it all. All the theory, all the history, all the spells, all the potions, and that knowledge, along with my weak magic, made me somewhat useful.

But I still hadn't discovered my affinity.

Hazel, did you get it?

Suppressing a groan, I placed the fist-sized white crystals on each corner of the six-pointed star. I looked around one more time, making sure nobody was in the alley or watching me through the windows, and stepped into the circle.

The energy from the crystals flowed into me and I opened my arms, welcoming that bit of extra magic. It rushed through my veins, bringing energy, life, and power. I smiled.

"*Veni ad me,*" I chanted, funneling my power. I sent my magic to all four corners. I felt it when it bumped into the other force, enveloped it, and pulled it to the circle. "Now you're mine."

The force struggled against me, but my magic was

strong when backed up by the crystals. The force crossed the circle's barrier and my magic released it. Immediately, it tried to step out of the circle. I almost laughed at its foolish attempts.

I channeled my powers. "*Apparet.*"

The air shimmered and smoke appeared, slowly forming the outline of a person. It was a ghost. I knew it.

"Hazel Rose Levine."

I snapped my head toward the voice and lost my grasp on my magic. The power of the crystals faded and the ghost vanished.

"Shit," I muttered.

A tall woman wearing a heavy white cloak with silver embroidery stood a good fifteen feet from the circle. The magic within her was so powerful that I could feel it brushing against my skin, filling the alley, chasing away ghosts.

A small brown owl appeared at the mouth of the alley, seated on top of a closed garbage can. It hooted once, and somehow I just knew this owl was a familiar.

I stepped out of the circle. "Yes?"

She took off the hood, revealing a plain face with sharp lines. Still, she was beautiful in an imposing, strong way. "I'm Lenora, one of the witches from the Lightgrove coven."

My throat became instantly dry and my hands damp. Lenora ... she was one of the council members of the Lightgrove coven. What was she doing here? I could only think of one thing.

"Um, have you received my request?" The one I had

sent two months ago, when I first arrived in New Orleans for summer classes. Several options had rolled through my mind since then. One, they didn't get my request. Two, they got it, and knowing how weak I was, chose to ignore it. Three, they got it and were spying on me, waiting to see if I should be granted an audience or not.

"We did," she said, her voice grave. "We decided it's time for us to meet."

My heart skipped a beat. I truly wasn't expecting this. "Really?"

She went on as if the excitement in my tone didn't amuse her one bit. "Tomorrow evening. At the appointed place and time." She waved her hand and an old, rolled parchment blinked into existence right in front of my face. I snatched it. "Don't be late."

"I won't," I promised.

She turned, but then stopped and looked around the tall buildings before her eyes settled back on me. "You should be careful, walking alone in the middle of the night. New Orleans is full of supernaturals, and most of them don't have good intentions."

I gulped. I had heard that, of course, but so far, I hadn't encountered any supernaturals, besides the one or two I knew about. But if she was warning me, then I should take it to heart.

The owl hooted again. Before I could answer, shadows surrounded her, and just like that, she was gone—and her familiar too.

A thrill bubbled in my chest, and I reached for my phone from over my tote. I began typing a text for my sister then stopped. What the hell? Who cared if it was past midnight? My mother would want to know this no matter the hour.

She answered on the second ring. "They contacted you?" she asked, her voice alert.

I frowned. "How did you know?"

"Calling me at this time? That better be it."

The excited feeling died down and I sighed. To her, that was the main reason I moved from our tiny town of Oak Hill, middle of nowhere in Louisiana, to New Orleans. No matter how much I wanted to go to college and live a normal life, since apparently I wasn't cut out for the witch thing. But she had made me promise, she begged me, to contact the Lightgrove coven, to request an audience so I could introduce myself and also request a position within their ranks.

"It would be the biggest honor," she had said.

Yes, it would. With the exception of my mother and Amanda, our family was the weakest in our entire region, and I was the weakest of them all. She would love to have a daughter inside the Lightgrove coven, the strongest, most powerful coven of light witches in existence. To my mother, I could be there as a maid. She didn't care as long as I got in.

"So," she asked. "When will you meet them?"

"Tomorrow." That was in less than twenty-four hours. My stomach knotted. I picked up the crystals and stashed them inside my tote. "I'll call you once I'm out."

"Please, Hazel …" She sighed. "Impress them somehow."

How was I supposed to do that? My magic didn't hold a candle to theirs. There was nothing I could do that would impress them. Honestly, I didn't know why they accepted my request.

I counted to ten before answering. "I'll try." I waved my hand to the circle. The red and white lines turned to dust that drifted away in the soft breeze.

"If they ask you for a demonstration, what will you do?"

I scanned the alley one more time, making sure I hadn't forgotten anything, then turned on the heels of my high-tops and walked out the alley.

"I don't know, mayb—" I bumped into something and tripped backward, but recovered before my butt met the ground. My phone fell from my hand, and my tongue tingled with curses. "What the f—?" I cut my words short and stared at the guy before me with wide eyes.

Even peering out from under a hood, his eyes pulled me in. He was breathtaking. His eyes were the brightest blue I had ever seen, and they went well with his fair skin and his dark brown hair, which was shaved close on the sides and longer on the top, but he didn't leave it up in spikes like Mohawks or fauxhawks. His puckered lips and sharp chin and jaw added to his beauty. As if his face wasn't enough, he was tall and wide. Peeking from his sleeveless hoodie, his arms were inked and toned, and right now, gleaming with sweat. I didn't know what to stare at first. The tattoos or the muscles or the sweat running over his skin.

Frowning, Hot Tattooed Guy bent down and picked up

my phone from the ground. "Sorry," he said, offering the phone to me.

I forced myself to swallow. "Thanks." I put the phone to my ear and flinched when I heard my mother yelling my name. "I'm here. I'm here. Sorry. I dropped the phone."

Hot Tattooed Guy stared at me the same way I had stared at him. Was he checking me out or was he simply curious about my unusual visual? My fair skin and pale blue eyes were nothing new. But blond hair streaked in red, a bar on my left eyebrow, a tiny crystal piercing in my nose (I had another, not so tiny, on my belly button, but he couldn't see that one), eyeliner and mascara, but no other kind of makeup, a tattoo of three stars on the side of my neck (I had more, but he also couldn't see those) were almost always something people stared at. Not to mention the style of clothes I liked. At the moment, I wore a thin, off-white, short-sleeved tee, black leggings, black and red high-tops, and had my red leather jacket hanging from my tote. Well, my style might have been a novelty back home, but I knew it wasn't here in New Orleans. Maybe he was staring at me for another reason, then. People always told me I looked younger than I was. Did he see me as a fifteen-year-old girl instead of eighteen?

His eyes met mine and I inhaled deeply. "Um, Mom. Can I call you tomorrow?"

"Sure," she said, sounding a little suspicious.

"Bye." I turned off the call before she could say anything else. I dropped my phone inside my tote. "Sorry about bumping into you."

Hot Tattooed Guy buried his hands in the pockets of

his sweatpants. "It's okay." His voice was deep and gruff. I told my girly side to be quiet before I acted like a hormonal high school girl and giggled at him. "It was my fault too. I should have been paying attention to where I was going."

"It's okay," I muttered. For some reason, I wanted to make him talk more. "I'm Hazel." I stretched my hand to him.

Hot Tattooed Guy glanced at my hand before taking it and enveloping mine in a firm handshake. "Sean."

My hand seemed so small in his. My cheeks warmed and I pulled my hand back. Trying to sound nonchalant, I tilted my head to the side, and said, "So, Sean, you run at this time of night?"

"And you talk on the phone with your mother in dark alleys?" he said, his tone tight. I almost flinched. He averted his eyes. "Sorry. It isn't my business."

"Yeah, well, sorry I asked too." As much as it pained me, I turned around and started walking to my dorm building.

The breeze blew again, carrying one of the many flyers spread throughout campus announcing the big welcoming party next weekend. Like everything in New Orleans, it would be one big costume party, and even though the dorms had started filling up two days ago, everyone was already talking about it. I stepped on the flyer and I picked it up, thinking about throwing it away in the next trash can I saw.

I took another three steps before Sean said, "Yes, I was running."

I stopped and glanced over my shoulder. Sean's body was angled toward me. Now he wanted to talk? I turned back. "Do you always run at this time of night?"

"Only when I can't sleep." He paused and touched a red macramé bracelet around his wrist. "Which is often."

"Oh." I wanted to ask why. Why couldn't he sleep? But I had never seen this guy before, and right now, he intrigued me. I neither wanted to pry too much or risk pushing him away, but I wanted to keep talking to him, even though I wasn't sure what to say.

"How about you?" he asked, surprising me. He looked like the quiet, lonely type. Making small talk wasn't his thing. "Do you always sneak into dark alleys and call your mother at this time of night?"

I smiled. Turning my own question against me. Touché. "Sometimes."

His expression hardened, and the muscles in his neck and shoulders tensed. "You shouldn't be out alone so late. It's dangerous."

On instinct, I took a step back. Was he warning me he was dangerous? Not that I was afraid. I really wasn't. I had ways of defending myself. A normal human would never touch me if I didn't want them to. But he didn't know that.

"Right," I said, playing along. "Well, classes start early tomorrow morning. I should get some sleep." I took another step back.

He nodded. "Good night."

"Good night," I said before walking the short distance to my building's front door.

Once inside, I spied on him through one of the lobby

windows. Sean remained in place, staring at my building door. Slowly, his gaze shifted up—to the dorm windows? He shook his head, turned around, and pushed into a run again.

I watched until I couldn't see him anymore. Sean was intriguing, to say the least.

I peeked at the flyer in my hand. It would be nice to go to the welcoming party. To go out, period. I spent most of my weekend nights hunting ghosts and putting them to rest. A welcoming party on a Friday the Thirteenth wouldn't be any different.

Fishing my phone from my tote, I climbed up the steps to my floor. There were several messages from Amanda. As much as I wanted to answer her, I really should go to sleep. Just because I was a witch, it didn't mean I didn't get tired, and knowing me, tomorrow I would feel like a zombie.

2

———

THE NEXT MORNING, I DID LOOK LIKE A ZOMBIE. IF I CARED about what others thought, I would have applied more makeup to hide the dark circles under my eyes. But since I didn't care, I played with the eyeliner and mascara as usual.

The first thing that popped in my mind once I opened my eyes was the encounter with Sean. I didn't know what to make of that. He was so ... hot? Handsome? Manly? Mysterious? Intriguing? There was more to him than he wanted people to see, and that made me curious.

The second thing on my mind was the audience. Holy shit, I had an audience with the Lightgrove witches later tonight. My stomach rolled and nervousness made its way into my system. Now I would spend the next handful of hours anxious and overthinking it.

The bathroom door slipped from my hand and closed with a bang. I held my breath, but my roommate only snored in her bed. I had met Krissa two days ago when she moved into our bedroom, but from the way she had barely stopped in here, I already knew she was a party girl. One of the only things she told me was that she never signed up for any classes that started before noon. This was officially my first semester at Towland University, since summer didn't count—I had taken two core classes then, and they had been in the middle of the morning. I made the mistake of picking some 8 a.m. classes. I had gone to bed past two in the morning, and I was starting to regret it.

As quiet as I could so I wouldn't wake her up, I got dressed in a thin black tee, my red leather jacket, skinny jeans, and black high-tops, and exited the room.

Towland was a big private school with almost fifteen thousand students. I could never have dreamed of being accepted into it, because of the requirements, and if it weren't for the handsome scholarship I had gotten I couldn't have afforded the tuition. Being a straight-A student with lots of extracurricular activities, which usually interested the admission committee of any university, had paid off.

On my way to my class, I stopped by the coffee shop, strategically placed at the center of campus. Thankfully, the line wasn't long and I was soon ordering my white mocha latte and a blueberry muffin.

Jane was the one preparing my drink. "How is it going?" she asked in a chipper voice.

I had known Jane for years now. She was two years older and from my hometown, and her family was a mix of humans and witches. She was half-witch, which I knew bothered her. From what I remembered, she had always wanted to be a full witch with incredible powers. But her family was as weak as mine, and being a half-witch made her powers even more ridiculous than mine.

I shrugged. "Can't complain." The news that I had an audience with the Lightgrove coven that night bubbled in my throat, but I pushed the words back down. This was something that would only make her sad, or even jealous.

Jane handed me my muffin and leaned over the counter. "You know, I sensed a ghost around the east dorms last evening," she whispered. "But ... um, I'm not strong enough to actually locate it or summon it."

I frowned. Could it be the same ghost I had tried to capture last night? I hadn't sensed any others in the last two days, and the only other one I had found during the summer, I had dealt with. Even though my dorms were on the south side of campus, ghosts were known to roam.

"I've sensed it too," I told her. "I'll take care of it."

With a tight smile, Jane gave me my coffee. "Great. Have a good day."

"You too."

I walked away, feeling bad about this exchange. Yeah, it had been a good idea not telling her about my audience with the Lightgrove coven.

For a minute, I pondered the ghost. If it was the same one, I would take care of it tonight. If it wasn't, I would find out and deal with it too.

I ate my muffin and drank my latte on my way to my literature class. It was a second-year class, but since I had taken other English classes during the summer, I qualified for it.

I was seated right in the middle of class when Sean walked in. He wore an open dark gray hoodie over a black T-shirt, and jeans. He had the hood pulled over his head. His eyes met mine and I held my breath. I raised my hand to wave at him, but he averted his eyes and marched to his seat at the back of the class.

I spied on him over my shoulder. He was looking down, at the cover of his closed book on his desk. Disappointment bloomed in my chest. Wasn't he curious about me like I was curious about him? I was so plain, so boring that he wouldn't even look at me?

"Careful," a girl said. I turned to the side. She was seated at the desk next to mine. "He's a handful."

I frowned. "Excuse me?"

"Sean Flaherty." She nodded her chin in his direction. "You were just staring at him, weren't you?"

I opened my mouth but nothing came out. "Hmm."

She continued before I could form a coherent sentence. "He's a mess after what happened."

"What happened?"

Her eyes bugged. "You haven't heard?"

"Heard what?"

She probably thought I was a sophomore like most students in here, but apart from summer, I was practically brand new at Towland.

The girl leaned over her desk. "Last year, he was a sophomore and one of the most popular guys on campus," she said in a low voice. "His younger sister and his best friend died on Halloween night. He was with them, and I heard he couldn't explain what happened. He got arrested since nobody knew how both of them died. They thought it could have been him, but he was found not guilty. He didn't come back to school and failed that semester, then he skipped spring and summer. He came back this semester, but from what I heard, he isn't the same. He avoids everyone." She glanced at him. "If you ask me, I would say his head is pretty messed up."

The professor walked in, and the girl straightened in her seat and turned her attention to the front. Not two minutes later, the professor began his lecture. My attention, however, was on the guy sitting in the back.

3

ON MONDAYS, I HAD FOUR CLASSES. MY FIRST ONE HAD BEEN literature, where I had seen Sean—and my mind had focused on him. But my last two, history and biology, had been a blur. My nervousness only grew as the day went by. My mind came up with several scenarios, none of which ended well. In one of them, the witches asked me to perform my most powerful spell, and I ended up setting the place on fire—not that I could have done that. Fire was harmful to light witches and no one could conjure fire.

In another scene, they were cruel and rough. They decided I was a shame to the entire witch race and that I could serve as a sacrifice. Which was ridiculous since they were light witches, not dark ones. As far as I knew, light witches were kind and fair, and they didn't perform sacrifices.

I stopped by my dorm, looked at myself in the mirror, and wondered if I should change clothes, maybe put on something more formal. What the hell? I wouldn't change to please them. The important thing—my magic—was already weak. My appearance wouldn't matter. I was going because I had to try for my mother.

I knelt beside my bed and waved my hand under it. A wooden box with ancient runes carved on the lid appeared, and I pulled it out. I opened it and ran my fingertips on my grimoire. It was thick with theory. If only I could do everything written in it. Or even half. Or one quarter. I would be more powerful than Amanda and my mother combined. I shook my head. What was I thinking? Hadn't I decided I wasn't cut out for this witch thing? This meeting was my last attempt, and after that, I was done. Even hunting ghosts and putting an end to their suffering. I would be done. I would be a normal girl going through college and planning my career.

A longing hit me as I ran a finger over the grimoire's spine. There was a time when I had wanted to be a witch. That had been years ago, when I had been hopeful and couldn't wait for my magic to manifest.

That didn't last long, though.

I opened my grimoire and skimmed through the thick pages. The first thing every witch learned was about our origins. To be fair, no one knew how supernaturals came to be, but many thousands of years ago, several witches with different powers founded the covens: Wildthorn, Bluemoon, Blackmarsh, Silverblood, Ravensoul, Crystalflame, Lightmist, and many others. To create their covens, the witches had magically taken out their hearts and enchanted them. It had become a priceless relic, one that powered the witches' magic. Each coven protected the hearts of the first witches of their covens with their lives.

These covens spread out through the world, hiding from predators and humans. Smaller covens showed up here and there.

About seven hundred years ago, Arianna became what was known as the most powerful Lightmist witch ever, even more powerful than their founder. However, she had discovered many of the Lightmist witches were deviating from their mission of being good witches, or what they called light witches. A large group of Lightmist witches didn't care about hiding from humans, about abusing their powers, about using humans and lesser supernaturals for their own good, and helping the world be a better place. They were greedy and powerful, and they wanted humans to become their slaves.

Arianna tried turning these witches back around, but soon she realized there was no reasoning with evil. So, she took the heart of the first Lightmist witch and officially changed their name to Lightgrove. She banished the dark witches from her coven. These dark witches founded the Darkmist coven. Their founder took out her heart and created the same spell as the previous witches, but it was said it didn't work. The founder died and her heart shriveled. The rumor was that the dark witches might have created a new coven for themselves, but their power was still tethered to the heart of the Lightgrove coven.

Also, when Arianna founded the Lightgrove coven, she distanced her new coven from the other covens, not just dark witches. She wanted the light witches to remain untainted by the influence of other witches.

However, with time, the Lightgrove coven grew and the council started being selective about the witches who were part of the coven. The other witches could live as humans, or create smaller covens of their own—without a heart, because technically, they were still tied to the Lightgrove coven.

As far as I knew, the Lightgrove witches were different from the other big covens. I had heard the Wildthorn witches lived close to a forest and had a great connection with nature, and the Blackmarsh witches had sacrifices to feed the heart of their coven and keep it powerful.

One other reason that made Arianna want to separate the light witches from the dark ones was the Brotherhood of Purity. The Brotherhood had been founded by the church, and it was almost as old as the most ancient witch coven. Its mission was to hunt witches who the Brotherhood believed had gained their powers from the devil. Dark witches had tainted the reputation of all witches, and the Brotherhood hunted innocent witches and killed them. Since then, the Brotherhood had evolved from being under the control of the church, but they still hunted us, especially Lightgrove and Darkmist witches, under the pretense that they were doing so for God.

Thankfully, I had never seen a Brotherhood member in his crimson cloak face-to-face, but I had heard chilling stories about the order's hunts. You would think we were still living in the dark ages.

A shudder rolled down my spine.

Carefully, I pulled the parchment Lenora had given me from under my grimoire, folded it until it was small enough to fit in the back pocket of my jeans, then closed the box, pushed it under the bed, and cast the cloaking spell again—I didn't want my roommate to accidentally find my witchy stuff.

With a last glance back to make sure everything was in its place, I opened the door and left for the most important appointment of my life.

4

THE INSTRUCTIONS ON THE PARCHMENT TOOK ME TO AN antiques store in the French Quarter. I glanced at the parchment, then back at the three-story building, crammed between a coffee shop and an apothecary. Intricate framework adorned the gallery on the second and third floor, and crystal chandeliers could be seen from big floor-to-ceiling windows. This couldn't be it, could it?

Certain I was in the wrong place, I entered the store. It was like any other antiques store. Too dark, too crammed with all kinds of crap, and hard to walk through. I weaved my way to the end of the store, where a blonde woman was writing something in a notebook at a desk.

"Hi, hmm, I think I'm lost, bu—"

She lifted her eyes to me and a small smile took over her lips. "Hazel Rose Levine," she said, her voice flat.

"Wait." I frowned. "Am in the right place?"

"The council is waiting for you." She beckoned me to a closed door behind her. She opened it. "Come."

Swallowing my nervousness, I forced one foot after the other and walked through the door. I turned to wait for the woman to come with me, show me where I was supposed to go, but she just smiled at me again and closed the door in my face. Darkness surrounded me.

I rested a hand on the cold wood. "Hey," I called. "What am I supposed to do now?"

She didn't answer. I twisted the knob, but it was locked. Damn it. Getting a grip on the fear wanting to crawl up my spine, I leaned my back against the door and took a deep breath. Okay. I could do this; whatever this was.

I extended my right hand in front of me. "*Lux.*"

A small white light appeared in my palm, shining bright but not enough to show me the end of the long, narrow hallway I was in. So far, I couldn't see any doors, just metal sconces every few feet, holding torches ready to be lit.

I forced myself to move forward. I tried controlling my nerves, but after walking for a few minutes and having reached no end, desperation clawed at my chest.

Trying something new, I duplicated the light in my hand and threw it ahead. It illuminated the walls as it rushed through the hallway, until it was too far away, and even I couldn't see its light anymore. Where the hell was I?

Then it hit me. This was a test.

I took in several deep breaths, trying to calm down. I was good at tests—when they didn't require a powerful witch. However, my mind was clear, and I was good with strategies. I knew all the theory. Now, I just needed to figure out what the light witches wanted me to do.

I looked around. Long hallway, walls, and the torches.

Hmm. I sent the light in my palm to the torch right in front of me. One by one, all the other torches lit up, creating a white haze in the long hallway. It went on and on, until I couldn't see it anymore. The fire on the torches grew, shining brightly. The walls became white. The ceiling and the floor became white. Too white. Too bright. I lifted my hand to my eyes, protecting them from the light.

A second later, the lights were gone. I dropped my arm and opened my eyes. I was back at the first door, and now the hallway was a few feet long, with only two sconces decorating the plain walls, and a second door at the end.

Suspicious, I reached for it and slowly turned the knob. It opened easily and I stepped through.

I gasped.

Smooth stone under my feet, green grass around it, darkening skies over my head, and a huge white castle right in front of me—the Light Castle. I turned around but the door was gone. Instead, I was at the edge of a forest. What the ...?

Six men stood before the closed gates of the castle, dressed in light-gray leather armor and white cloaks, and a metallic baton hanging from their waists. One of them stepped forward and I instantly stepped back.

"Hazel Rose Levine," he said. "The council is waiting for you."

The gates rose and the guards formed a living corridor, waiting for me to pass. Wishing I had brought the crystals in my purse in case I needed to use magic to defend myself, I walked down the stone path, crossing the gates into a beautiful front garden. A dozen steps led to double doors that looked too big, too heavy to be opened without magic.

I put my foot on the first step and the doors opened. Wearing a simple but beautiful blue gown, Lenora appeared from behind it. "Hazel Rose Levine, welcome." Her owl was perched on the doorway behind her.

Familiars weren't common among *normal* witches. Only the most powerful light and dark witches had them.

"Hi." I climbed the rest of the steps. "Hmm, you don't need to keep calling me by my full name. Just Hazel is fine."

Her expression didn't change. "Just Hazel. This way, please."

She led me through an imposing foyer, around a colorful winter garden, in front of stairs that seemed out of a movie, down a long corridor with floating white flames for light—her owl followed us the entire way. Guards were strategically placed at archways and in front of doors—all of them impassive and with their hands close to the silver baton at their waist.

This place was impossible. It couldn't be located in New Orleans. There was no way I wouldn't have known of its existence if it were.

Finally, the corridor ended at another set of large double doors. Lenora waved her hand and the doors opened. Following her, I entered a big room with ten white chairs forming a circle. She positioned me in the center, and I couldn't help but squint at several markings on the stone floor.

"Arianna's marks," I whispered.

"That's right," a new voice said. I raised my head and was taken aback. Half of the chairs were now occupied. A woman with long raven hair and wearing a light yellow gown smiled. Pinned to the bodice of her gown was a white pentagram brooch with a rune in the center—the Lightgrove symbol. Behind her, perched on the chair, was a red bird. Her familiar. "What do you know about Arianna?"

I stilled but forced my voice out. "I—I know that she was the most powerful light witch who ever lived, and that around seven hundred years ago, she founded the Lightgrove coven."

"You're right," the woman said. "How did she die?"

Was this another test? To know the history of the light witches? If it was, it was a boring test. "Her village was surrounded by the Brotherhood of Purity. Prince Thales arranged for some of his men to take Arianna out of town, but unfortunately, the soldier, Hugo, betrayed the prince and brought Arianna directly into a trap. Prince Thales arrived as Arianna was dying. He killed the men who captured her, but it was too late. She died in his arms, becoming ashes right after. Some rumors tell that Prince Thales gathered Arianna's ashes, and he spent the rest of his life trying to bring her back to life, but he failed."

Thinking about Arianna's body and ashes, I realized I was in the freaking Light Castle and somewhere in here, the heart of the first Lightmist witch was hidden. Locked away and heavily protected. It was a strange feeling, knowing I was so close to such a powerful object.

"Those aren't rumors." The woman entwined her long fingers and rested her hands on her lap. "It's all true. Prince Thales spent the rest of his short life trying to find Arianna's grimoire and necklace, so he could bring her back to life. Because of the pain of losing her, he established the Light Order, so the men who loved the Lightgrove witches would be best equipped to protect them. In between his quest to find Arianna's possessions, he oversaw the Light Order's training himself. But not even seven years after Arianna's death, Prince Thales perished during one of his expeditions. We know the sisters Brita and Anna, Arianna's friends, buried him in a hidden, unmarked grave with Arianna's ashes right before they were burned at the stake themselves."

I remembered having read about Brita and Anna before. After Arianna's death, they helped Prince Thales, but the three of them failed. The sisters couldn't even save Thales when his end came. Back in their hometown, the sisters were accused of being evil, of meeting with the devil and doing his bidding. They had been caught by the Brotherhood of Purity, and for some reason, they didn't run away; they didn't fight it. The sisters were burned at the stake for the public to witness.

I nodded. "Why are you telling me all this?"

The woman's smile widened. "Everything we talk about here, everything you see here, is part of your test."

I felt the blood rushing out of my face. So there would be a real test. I was doomed. "Oh."

"Welcome, Hazel. I'm Queen Denise," the woman said, serious now. I gaped at her, taking her in. So this was the famous Witch Queen Denise of the Lightgrove coven. Of course, I had heard of her before. If a light witch hadn't, then she wasn't really a light witch.

"It's a pleasure to meet you," I finally said.

Queen Denise gestured to the witch on her right, a beautiful woman with red hair, wearing a white dress. "This is Clara." Then she pointed to an older witch with graying hair and wearing a dark green dress on her left side. She also had a familiar, a dark green snake which was wrapped around the chair's feet. "This is Grace." The queen moved on to a woman with dark skin and curly brown hair, wearing a light pink gown, seated at Grace's left. "This is Amelia." She motioned to the last one. "And I believe you already met Lenora." I nodded, noticing they all wore the same white brooch. "We're the council of the Lightgrove."

"I— It's an honor to be here," I said, feeling very, very lame.

"You requested an audience with us back in June, correct?" Queen Denise asked.

"Yes. The first week of June." It was when I had arrived in New Orleans for summer classes.

"I apologize we took so long to contact you," Queen Denise continued. "As you may imagine, we're very busy here and we like to do research about the witches wanting to see us." Oh, here it came. "Your bloodline is weak, and you're weaker than most. However, we think you have potential. We sense there's more in you."

"What?"

"Tell us about the first time your powers manifested," Lenora said.

I frowned. "My mother was teaching Amanda a mild healing potion, and I was in the back, observing. After she was done with the potion, Amanda knocked the vial off the table. The ingredients were hard to come by. It would have been a shame to waste it. On instinct, I reached for it, but I was too far away. I would never get to the vial in time. To my surprise, the vial stopped in midair. At first, I thought it was Amanda, but she said she wasn't doing anything. Waving my hand, I brought the vial up and back to the table."

Queen Denise shook her head. "Not that time. We're talking about the first time your magic manifested." She paused. "When you were nine."

A chill ran through my spine. "How ...?"

She offered me a small smile. "We know everything. Tell us."

I had never told this tale to anyone, not even my mother or my sister. In fact, I had forced myself to forget about it, to push it away, to ignore it and pretend it never happened.

I gulped, willing my heartbeat to return to normal. "I was an odd kid. Too skinny and quiet. I liked reading and science. I was picked on by bullies all the time. There was this girl. She was two years older than me and a whole lot bigger. She loved pushing me, calling me names, just bothering me. She started stealing my lunch and throwing away my homework. One day, she was following me home, taunting me. I was carrying a Mother's Day gift I had made in school, proud of my artistic skills. She pushed me and I fell in the dirt, destroying the gift. I ... I don't know. I just reacted. I threw my hands at her. She flew several feet and fell on her back. But I didn't stop. With my magic, I lifted her up in the air and squeezed her throat. She was turning purple and that's when I realized what I was doing. I ... I almost killed her. I stopped and she ran away, yelling I was a freak." It had been terrible. The girl spread rumors at school, and then all the kids called me freak. My sister didn't understand and she kept asking me about it, but I pretended I didn't know why they were picking on me.

"Did you try using your powers after that?" Queen Denise asked.

I sighed. "No. I was afraid of hurting someone else."

She nodded. "Your fear suppressed your magic, until you were sixteen and couldn't hold it back anymore. It slipped through your barrier, even though you didn't want it to."

Shame hurt my chest. "It's not that I didn't want it."

"I understand," Queen Denise said.

"Anyway," Lenora continued. "We'll give you a chance."

Forgetting about my depressing past, my heart soared. "Really?"

Queen Denise smiled. "All the witches who joined our coven had to prove themselves. You'll have to do the same."

Oh shit. "What do I have to do?"

Her smile faded. "In three days, the veil between the living world and the dead world will become thin."

Three days. "Friday the Thirteenth?"

Lenora nodded. "Yes, like All Hallows' Eve, Winter

Solstice, and other mystical events, Friday the Thirteenth is another day when the magic in the world acts up."

I knew about Halloween, but I had no idea about Winter Solstice and Friday the Thirteenth.

"The veil becomes so thin that it actually rips in several places, especially here in New Orleans," Queen Denise continued. "Many of our witches spend the night finding and patching the cuts in the veils, then sending the ghosts back to their side. That will be your job." She waved her hand and a rolled parchment popped in front of my face, much like Lenora did two days ago. I closed my hand around it. "Here's a list of places in New Orleans where the veil will most likely rip. Close as many cuts as you can, send as many ghosts back as you can, and we'll talk later about your performance."

I gulped. So it wasn't a do-this-and-you'll-pass kind of test. It was a do-this-and-we'll-talk-about-it one. I was nervous because I wanted to please them, not because of how hard the test was. I had been sending ghosts back to their side for a long time. However, I had never closed a cut or sent a bunch of ghosts back at the same time. I wasn't sure I could do it, not with how weak I was, but I sure would try.

"Report back here on Saturday by noon. Do you understand the terms of your test, Hazel?" Queen Denise asked.

I cleared my throat. "Yes."

"You should also know, all witches who pass the test don't immediately join our ranks," Lenora said. "But we can discuss more about this later."

What did she mean they didn't join immediately? I

wanted to ask more about this, but I felt like I wouldn't get an answer, no matter what. "Sure," was all I said.

"You're dismissed," Queen Denise said. "Good luck."

As if they had comprehended her words, the double doors opened. Lenora stood from her chair and led me back to the front of the castle.

"Good luck," she said from atop the front steps.

"Thanks." I walked down the stairs, through the garden and under the gate. I stopped for a moment and gawked again at the magnificent Light Castle. It could be the second to last time I saw it, and I wanted to keep it in my memories.

Sighing, I turned away and faced the edge of the forest.

A guard dressed all in white came to my side. He extended his hand between two trees and the door appeared between the trunks. He opened it for me. "Good luck," he said, a small smile stretched over his lips, accentuating the tiny scar on the corner of his mouth. If he hadn't smiled, I wouldn't have seen it.

I nodded, knowing I would need way more than luck to help me with this test.

5

On my way back to campus, I opened the notes app on my phone and started a list of things I would need. Since I wasn't powerful enough alone, I would need potions, lots of potions, of all kinds, to help me on the task.

I also called my mother. Of course, she squealed loud enough to almost burst my eardrum. I wanted to ask for advice, but it would go to her head, and she would stay on the phone with me until tomorrow morning, probably telling me stuff I already knew. I knew her grimoire, her mother's grimoire, her grandmother's grimoire, and Amanda's grimoire by heart. What else could she tell me that I didn't know?

At the top of my list was a trip to the Midnight Cauldron tomorrow after class. The witch doctor there would have all the ingredients I needed, and she would probably know a thing or two about Friday the Thirteenth and ghosts in New Orleans.

I was walking to my dorm building when I saw Sean

leaning against the wall of the building next to mine, in the mouth of the same alley where I was trying to catch a ghost yesterday. His leg was propped up, his foot on the wall, and a cigarette in his hand. His face, half hidden under the hoodie, was turned up, his eyes fixed on a window or a spot on the wall on the third or fourth floor.

What was he doing here? Perhaps he was waiting for a girl. For some reason, a little jealousy made its way into my chest. I should play it cool and ignore him, like he did to me in class this morning, but I couldn't help it.

I walked up to him. "You were running yesterday, and now you're smoking. Isn't that, like, opposites?"

He turned his face to me, his bright blue eyes piercing mine, and his expression flat. "At least I run."

I glanced at the spot he seemed to be staring at. "Are you waiting for someone?"

He frowned. "What?"

"You were looking up as if you were waiting to see someone, or waiting for someone to come down."

He took a long drag of his cigarette, and then let the smoke out of his mouth slowly before answering. "No. No. I'm just ..." He trailed off, not finishing whatever was on his mind.

The power from the other night fleeted through the alley, and I snapped my head toward it, sure that it was stronger now. Shit. If Sean weren't here, I would have entered the alley and tried contacting it, even without drawing the circle and placing the crystals.

I turned my back to the alley, trying as hard as I could to ignore the ghost.

The welcome party poster was stapled to a frail tree along the sidewalk. I opened my mouth and was about to ask him if he was going to the party, but I remembered what the girl in class told me about him. If he was still grieving the deaths of his sister and his friend, I bet he wouldn't go.

I wished I knew more about what happened. Where were they exactly? How did she die? I wished I could help him with his grief. I wished there was a spell to bring back the dead, or to make someone forget, or at least to take away the pain. Well, there were spells for some, but none of those were viable options.

Sean followed my line of sight. "Are you going to the party?"

"N-no."

"Why? No one asked you out yet?" he asked. I tilted my head, wondering what he meant. He must have seen it in my face, because he averted his eyes and said, "I mean, guys must have asked you, right? You're too beautiful to ignore. Then, what? You said no because the one you want hasn't asked you yet?"

Wait. Pause. He thought I was too beautiful to ignore? Where'd that come from? "N-no, I'm not waiting for anyone to ask me out. And I wouldn't mind going alone, if that were the case. I just ... I don't go to parties much."

He returned his eyes to mine. He took another pull off his cigarette before throwing it on the ground and stomping on it. "I'm not a partygoer either. I used to be, though."

Great opening for me to ask him more about it,

without actually pushing the subject too hard, if it weren't for the freaking power in the alley, floating around, growing stronger then weaker, stronger then weaker. Teasing me as if daring me to follow it. I glanced over my shoulder. If the ghost wanted, it could let us see it. I prayed it didn't. I didn't need a damaged Sean to be even more damaged.

The power zipped across the air and rushed to my building through a window on the fourth floor.

"Everything all right?" Sean asked.

I turned back to him and forced a small smile. "Yeah, sure. I just ... I have stuff to do. Homework and a project." I took a step back. "See you around?"

Sean nodded, burying his hands in the pockets of his jeans. Without another word, he turned his back to me and walked away. Retreating to my building's door, I watched his tall, nicely framed figure until he rounded a corner and was gone.

I sighed.

The power inside the building spiked, and I rushed inside, following it until I was in front of a closed dorm door on the fourth floor. Room 408. Voices were coming from inside. Damn it.

Hoping no one would think I was creepy, I leaned against the opposite wall and closed my eyes. I focused on my magic and said, "*Apparet*."

The power vanished.

I opened my eyes and stared at the closed door as if it held all the secrets I needed to unveil. What the hell? Was my magic so weak that even the ghost found it pathetic and played with me?

The door opened and a blonde girl stepped out. She paused and spoke to someone else inside the room. "Okay. I'm just going to see if they have it in another color." She lifted her hand, gesturing to a paper bag she held. The bag was black with the logo of one of the biggest costume stores around. I could see the point of a purple witch hat peeking from it. "Be right back."

Not noticing me, she strolled down the hallway to the stairs. Her red-haired roommate poked her head around the door. "Hey, ask them if they have it in red. We could go to the party in matching costumes."

Halted at the edge of the stairs, the blonde nodded. "Great idea." They smiled at each other before moving on.

Hmm. An idea sprouted in my mind.

6

Even though it was almost noon on a Tuesday, I had
to sneak into my own room so I wouldn't wake up Krissa. If
I didn't need to change my books for my afternoon class, I
wouldn't even come in here, because if I wasn't careful
enough and accidentally woke up her up, she threw a giant
fit and screamed so the entire building could hear—I
knew. It had happened on Monday.

To my surprise, Krissa was already awake. Still in
bed, with her head propped up on two pillows and
messing on her phone with her eyes half-open, but
awake.

"Did you fall from bed?" I asked as I closed the door
behind me.

She groaned, but her fingers moved rapidly over her
phone as she typed something. I shrugged and walked to
my desk, where I put down my books and gathered the
ones I would need next. It was so much easier to be here
normally and not feeling like a mouse sneaking in.

Krissa looked up at me from her phone. "I didn't sleep well," she mumbled.

Shit. "Did I snore?"

She snorted. "If you do, I haven't heard it. Thank God!" I chuckled. "But seriously, I kept having weird dreams about ghosts."

I stilled. "Ghosts?"

"Yeah." She sat up on the bed and looked at me. "You'll think I'm crazy, but last night we were gathered in the common room of the Waller dorm on the east side of campus, partying as we usually do, and then one of the guys started telling us ghost stories. He said he had heard weird noises in his building, *that* building. He said he went to check the noise and found nothing. He just felt super cold and suddenly the lights flickered. We all thought he was messing with us, of course, but then it happened."

Krissa had my full attention now. "What happened?"

"Exactly what he said. The music cut off and weird noises echoed around us. Then it felt like someone had turned the AC on us. And then"—she moved her hands fast, almost shaking them— "the lights flickered! Everyone screamed there was a ghost and bolted."

"But no one saw anything?"

"Of course not!" Her lips pursed and she shook her head. "I don't know! I mean, ghosts aren't real, I know that, but that didn't feel like a prank, you know? I came back around two in the morning, but I couldn't sleep. Every time I closed my eyes, I imagined ghosts were circling our bedroom, waiting in the shadows to scare us."

"Hm." I frowned. A dorm on the east side of campus. It

was the same place Jane said she had felt a ghost. It couldn't be a coincidence. "You said the Waller dorm, right?"

"Yeah." Krissa pushed up from the bed. "I'm telling you, I don't care if it was a prank or not, it wasn't nice. I'm never going back there."

I raised my eyebrows at her. "Even if it's for a party?"

She glanced at me as she walked to the bathroom. "Even if it's for a party."

I seriously doubted that.

Krissa disappeared inside the bathroom and I mused about this ghost. Was it the same one I was hunting the other night? It could be. Glancing around, I opened my senses and tried calling for the ghost I had felt before. Not even a flicker.

I let out a sigh.

Oh, well, ghosts would have to wait, because right now, I had to go to class.

WHEN MY LAST CLASS OF THE DAY ENDED, I LEFT THE classroom with my phone in my hand. I stared at the screen and the multiple text messages from an unknown number.

Unknown: *Hey, it's Jane. I was at the dorm I told you about and I felt the ghost's presence.*

My steps faltered and I frowned. How the hell had she gotten my number? I glanced at the time stamp on her text. It hadn't been even thirty minutes ago. With a hand over my eyes, I looked up at the bright sky. It was only five thirty. I couldn't go there now. It was still too early and there would be too many students around. I had to wait until it was at least dark to go find a ghost.

But then I risked not finding the ghost at all.

However, the ghost had been there last night and this afternoon. The chances of finding it there in two hours seemed high.

To pass the time, I went back to my dorm, dropped off my books, took a shower, changed my clothes, and then went to the coffee shop to get a white mocha latte. As I expected, Jane was working behind the counter.

"You got my message?" she asked, as she started preparing my latte. I would regret having coffee this late in the day, but if I was to face a ghost in a few minutes, I needed some fuel.

"I did." I glanced out the window where the sun was finally falling behind the buildings. "I'm waiting until it's darker out, and then I'll check it out."

"Oh, I want to go with you."

I shook my head. "No, it's okay. You probably just started your shift, right?"

"Yeah, but it's okay. Susan owes me a favor." She handed me my latte. "Wait up. I'll talk to her."

I grabbed my drink as Jane raced to the back of the coffee shop where another girl was working on the stock, completely ignoring the three people in line behind me. I sighed, trying to think of an excuse. I really didn't want a sidekick, especially one who probably had never done this before and didn't even have enough magic to help me.

My brows curled down and I looked at my to-go cup. Wow, that was really shitty of me. I had no right to pass judgement, and I was sure there were many witches out there who probably thought even worse of me.

Well, if she wanted to come with me, it wasn't like I could stop her. I just hoped she did what I told her, which would probably be to stay back and let me handle it.

Jane had to work for another twenty minutes while Susan called in someone to fill in for her, which was fine with me. When her replacement arrived, Jane joined me outside, looking way too eager for someone who would go ghost hunting, probably for the first time.

With a smile from ear to ear, she bounced on the heels of her feet. "So, how does it work?"

I fought the urge to roll my eyes. Holy shit, this girl would get us killed tonight. "Just ..." I shook my head and beckoned her forward. "Let's go."

We started toward the east dorms. Earlier, I had looked at the campus map to make sure I knew exactly where the Waller building was located, but now with Jane, she could lead us.

As we walked, I thought of something. "How did you get my number?"

"Oh, I had my mother call your mother," she said, sounding proud of herself. Of course our mothers knew each other. Weak witches might not even belong to other covens, but they stuck together. Our mothers weren't close, but they had worked together before.

A chilly breeze blew by and I hugged my red jacket tighter. It was unusually cold for August in New Orleans.

Of course, the Waller building looked like mine, and every other dorm on campus, and as expected, a handful of students came in and out as night crept in. Some were leaving to meet their significant others or for midweek get-togethers, and others were retreating for the evening after a day full of classes.

Jane and I sat on a wooden bench just outside the building, as if we were waiting for someone. I glanced up at the many windows, opening my senses to the ghost.

It took me a moment, but I finally sensed it. Its faint energy was coming from somewhere on the first floor. "I can feel it," I told Jane.

Her eyes bugged. "You do?"

I nodded. "Let's go in."

She followed me inside the building. In the foyer, we passed by a girl who was going up the stairs. I walked slowly, listening for more steps, but I didn't see anyone else. Slowly, I advanced, letting the ghost's energy guide me.

"Where is it?" Jane whispered.

I halted in front of the media room's door. "In here, I think." I pressed my ear to the door, but didn't hear anything. It seemed there was no one inside, other than the ghost.

I reached for the knob when a shiver ran down my spine and a sleek, heavy feeling pressed against my back. Faint footsteps approached. On instinct, I grabbed Jane's hand and pulled her back, to the end of the corridor, where darkness prevailed, and we turned the corner, hiding against the wall.

"What is it?" she asked in a whisper.

I pressed a finger to my lips.

Holding my breath, I spied around the corner.

Two figures with long red cloaks walked down the corridor and stopped in front of the door to the media room.

My throat went dry.

These were members of the Brotherhood of Purity.

The two men looked at each other, then pushed open the door and stepped in.

Still holding Jane's hand, I turned to the other side of the corridor and raced to the next exit door. Jane stumbled after me, but didn't argue. We paused at the door, and I opened it carefully, glancing out. I couldn't see any Brotherhood members out there, but that didn't mean they weren't out there. I let go of Jane's hand, but gestured for her to come with me. We raced out of the building and didn't stop running until we were three blocks away and well within the busiest of the campus's buildings, where many humans still milled.

I took in a lungful of air, trying to calm my racing heart. But after what we had seen, there was no calming down.

Jane looked at me. "Were those ...?"

I nodded. "Brotherhood of Purity."

Her brow furrowed. "What were they doing here?" Suddenly, her face paled. "Do you think they were looking for witches?"

"I don't know," I said, my words low, my throat hurting. "They seemed to be going to the media room, where the ghost was."

"Now they hunt ghosts too?"

I shook my head once. I didn't know what to think, what to do. All my focus was on trying to steady my breathing, my shaking heads, my racing thoughts. Holy shit, I had never seen the Brotherhood of Purity up close and it terrified me. They were here, at Towland, within my corner of the world. What if Jane was right and they were looking for witches? She and I wouldn't be safe. Any witch trying to pass as human—and there were plenty—wouldn't be safe.

"I think ..." I inhaled deeply, focusing on what we should do next. What was the best action we could take now? But there wasn't much she and I could do. "I think we should retreat. Go to your dorm, I'll go to mine, and we lay low for the night. I won't go after that ghost for now." Or forever.

She nodded, her full fear on display in her big eyes. "Agreed." She looked back, in the direction of her dorm. "Wait ... hm, what if they find us?"

"They won't; they shouldn't." At least, that was what I was telling myself. "We've been on campus for a couple of months now. If they were here for us, we would know it already. No, they were here for something else." That ghost. But why? "Like I said, just lay low. Go to class, go to work, and done. At least for a handful of days."

She hesitated but nodded again. "Okay. Okay." Her eyes moved side-to-side. "All right. I'm off, then."

"Be careful," I told her.

"You too."

Then Jane turned and ran toward her dorm building.

And I stayed frozen in place for a moment, trying to understand what had happened. I fished my phone from my pocket, clutching it tight with my shaking hands, and stared at the screen.

The right thing to do at this moment was to contact the Lightgrove coven and let them know the Brotherhood of Purity was in Towland. But I didn't have their number. Did they even have a number? My only option to warn them was to go to the Light Castle, and I wasn't sure I would be welcome there without an invite.

The second thing I thought about was calling my mother, but how would that help? She would only freak out and that wouldn't be any help to anyone.

No, there was nothing I could do right now other than what I told Jane: lay low and wait for it to pass.

With that in mind, I held on to my bravado and made my way to my dorm, where I hid under the covers and didn't peek out until the next morning.

Wednesday was a busy day. I had two classes in the morning and two in the afternoon. According to Krissa, I was crazy for taking so many credits. She wasn't too far from the truth.

Throughout the day, I kept my head low and my eyes on the horizon, looking for threats. At moments, I thought I had imagined the Brotherhood members in that dorm, but I knew it had been real.

They had been here, right under my nose. How many other times had they been this close and I hadn't known? The thought was scary. I wished I had never known.

I shoved thoughts and fears of the Brotherhood to the back of my mind and tried to focus on acting as I always did. Here I was a human, a student interested in her classes, and nothing more.

After my classes, time passed in slow motion. If there were spells to stop or slow time, I would be sure someone was messing with me. But since there weren't—not that I knew of—the only thing to blame was my nerves. I had already gone through the meeting, why was I still nervous? Oh, let me see, because I had to prove to the light witches that I could do this and that I was worth joining their coven.

I was doomed.

I had planned to cook a quick dinner for myself at my dorm—Krissa was out with her friends, of course—but I was too fidgety to stay still. I needed to walk, to be around other people, to watch life. Maybe something would catch my attention, and I would forget about my test enough to relax a bit. I just didn't go to the Midnight Cauldron, because that would take a long time, and it really didn't matter if I went today or tomorrow—I had more time tomorrow.

I checked myself in the mirror, making sure my mascara and liner hadn't run, and that my hair wasn't all messed up, then grabbed my purse, made sure at least one of my crystals were in there, and left.

Students milled in the hallways and lobby of my building, probably planning on getting together for an early fun night. After all, we were in college in New Orleans. Who wasn't partying? Me, that was who. Instead, I hunted ghosts and went crazy overthinking an upcoming magical test.

Now, I also pretended I wasn't aware that the Brotherhood could be lurking in the shadows, ready to get me.

If the Brotherhood was lurking close by, what else could there be? Dark witches? Vampires? A shudder ran down my spine.

Stop it, Hazel. There's no use letting fear win.

Walking through campus, I tried not to let myself hope, but it was hard not to. I had heard about how glorious and rewarding the light witches' work was. Supposedly, it was much more than hunting ghosts—that was actually one small job they did when they had spare time. Supposedly, they were different from the other witches ... they were more reserved, more conscious, and cared about all supernaturals and humans alike. It was said this was another reason the Lightgrove coven didn't get along well with the other covens.

I sighed, turning a corner and walking off the university campus. The street was a French Quarter wannabe, with bars and restaurants and even a couple fake voodoo shops, and it housed a small diner with the best burger and fries I had ever tasted. At this time of the evening, the sidewalks were already bustling, and loud music could be heard from inside the bars, one competing with another.

Two buildings from the diner, a guy tripped out from a bar and bumped into me. My steps faltered and I almost fell in the street, if it weren't for the lamppost at my side and my bearlike grip on it.

"Hey!" I complained, but the guy didn't even notice me.

Instead, he rushed toward the entrance of the bar, letting out a growl. What the ...? Then Sean stepped out from inside the bar, meeting the guy head on. With a feral glint in his bright blue eyes, Sean lifted his fist and smashed the guy's jaw. The guy scrambled back, but recovered and landed a punch to Sean's stomach. Sean doubled over, and the guy took advantage and landed an uppercut to Sean's chin. People gathered around them on the sidewalk, watching the fight as if it were a show. Wouldn't anyone do anything to stop them?

I stepped forward. "Stop it," I called out. However, the hollers and the whistles of the crowd drowned my voice.

Sean kicked the guy in the side, and then punched his face again. I didn't know much about fighting, but Sean seemed like he knew what he was doing. Where the hell had he learned how to fight?

I walked closer. "Sean, stop it."

He didn't acknowledge me. He lunged at the other guy, landing another punch. Then the guy was on him again.

"Sean! Stop it!" I yelled.

That caught his attention. His eyes went wide as he stared at me. And that cost him. The guy punched his cheek so hard I swear I heard the bones cracking. Sean fell on his side on the sidewalk, grunting. The guy advanced on him, but I stepped in front of Sean and whispered, "*Praerigidus.*"

The guy's arms dropped to his side as if they weighed a ton. His legs wobbled, and soon he was on the ground too. "Help!" he shouted, unsure what was happening to him. It was a numbing spell. He would be back to normal in about fifteen minutes. A couple of guys knelt beside the numb guy, asking what was wrong.

The crowd booed me, and some even said I had disrupted their fun. Really?

I turned to Sean. He was propping up on his elbows, his face scrunched. I crouched beside him. "Are you okay?"

He opened his eyes in thin slits. "Do I look okay?"

I grabbed one of his arms. "Let me help you."

He jerked his arm away, and wincing and grunting, stood on his own. He looked at me with something like rage in his eyes. I didn't like it.

"What are you doing here?" he asked, his voice grating.

Unease assaulted me, and I put my hands inside the pockets of my jacket. "I was about to grab some dinner, but then I saw you. What happened?"

"Nothing," he barked. He took a step away from me and wobbled to the side. I caught his arm as if I was able to hold him up in case he went down. Again, he jerked his arm from my hold.

"Let me help you," I said, my tone low, careful. His nose was bleeding, his cheek was swollen, dark red, and soon would be black, and the skin above his left eyebrow had split. "I can help you. Please."

He groaned, but let me close. I put his arm over my shoulder and wound my arm around his back. He winced. On instinct, I lifted his hoodie and saw another red welt darkening the side of his stomach, right over a lot of well-defined muscles.

Gulping, I dropped the hoodie and focused on helping him. "Where to?"

He jerked his chin to the other side of the street. "This way."

Even though he limped and suppressed groans every two seconds, Sean led the way. He took me out of the busy street and three blocks north, to an old and beaten apartment building. He fished the keys from his hoodie pocket and unlocked the front door. Going up the stairs to the second floor was a little bit more complicated. He really didn't want me to see that he was in pain, so after the fifth step, I helped him. I used magic to give him a hand. It was like there was another me on his other side, lifting him up. Thankfully, he was too out of it to question anything.

He paused in front of apartment 2D. He disentangled himself from me, trying to stay on his feet without any support, and then he stared at me with cold eyes. "Thank you for your help."

A bucket of cold water in my chest. That was what his words felt like. "Oh." I didn't know why, but I thought he would invite me in, let me help him to his bed, look over his wounds, make sure he was really okay. Disappointment was a bitch. I stepped back. "Okay."

I turned and started down the hallway toward the stairs.

He cursed under his breath. "Hazel, wait." I halted and glanced over my shoulder. He ran a hand through his hair, and then flinched. "You ... do you want to come in?"

"I ... I don't want to impose."

Sean unlocked the door and pushed it open. "You won't impose."

He limped inside and I followed. I closed the door behind me while he slowly took off his hoodie. My attention was divided between taking in his toned arms or his place—no decorations, no bright colors, little furniture. Just a small loft with a worn sofa and TV on the left, a square dining table with a kitchenette to the right, and three doors past the living room, where I guessed the bedrooms and bathrooms were. The only decoration on the walls was a hanger hook with several belts of different colors. A black belt was on the right corner of the hook. So he was some kind of martial artist. Now his fighting skills made sense.

Sean threw his hoodie over the couch, revealing a white T-shirt that hugged his physique. Plus, his sweat made the T-shirt really stick to his skin, and it was hard not to stare.

He dragged his feet to the kitchen and reached for a cabinet. His hand dropped suddenly, and with a groan, he leaned on the counter.

I rushed to him. "What is it?" I halted three feet from him.

Slowly, he turned around and rested his back on the counter. He pressed a hand on the cut on his forehead. "Just a little dizzy."

I stepped into his personal space and snaked my arms around his waist. His eyes widened and he stilled. I sighed. What? Was it so bad to be touched by me? "Come on. I'll help you to your bed."

Sean shook his head. "The couch." He leaned into me, and once again, I used magic to help me carry him. As we walked the short distance to the couch, I tried focusing on my test, on my homework, on anything other than his warm, hard body glued to my side.

I helped him down, and grunting, he lay on the couch. He kicked his shoes off, propped his long legs on the couch's arm, and draped an arm over his eyes.

"Do you have a first aid kit? And medicine?"

"Medicine in the kitchen cabinet, and the first aid kit is in the bathroom," he said, his voice weak.

I found the first aid kit under the bathroom sink, and a shoebox with medicine in the kitchen cabinet he was reaching for moments before. I also grabbed a glass of water, and then returned to Sean's side. I crouched down and handed him two ibuprofens. He took them while I opened the first aid kit.

He spied on me under his arm. "There's no need for that."

"The cut over your eyebrow is open. Let me clean it."

I reached to his face, but he turned away. I placed my finger under his chin and guided his face back to me. He let me take his arm from over his eyes, the same ones that were staring at me with something like disbelief or wariness. Or maybe both.

"This might hurt a little."

I dabbed a cotton pad with antiseptic on his cut, and he hissed. My curiosity had been eating at me since I first saw him exit that bar and launch at that other guy. I tried putting it past me. It was none of my business, but being here, in his apartment, with him, with no one to overhear us or judge him, I couldn't hold it in any longer.

"Want to talk about what happened?"

A muscle in his jaw popped, and his fists clenched and unclenched. "Not really."

I slapped a Band-Aid on his cut. When I retreated, he touched the red bracelet on his wrist. "Does it mean anything?"

Sean lifted one shoulder, but remained quiet. All right.

He didn't want to talk. What did I think? That he would open up, let me in, tell me all his secrets, and let me help him?

And why the hell did I feel like I needed to help him? I didn't need this kind of drama.

Sighing, I stood. "Well, you're home, safe and more or less sound. See you in class tomorrow."

I turned and walked to the door. I didn't want to look back, but my will was weak and I did. Sean was staring at me with a big frown. When my eyes met his, he shifted on the couch—grunting—until his back was to me.

I nodded to myself, making a mental note to never mess with fucked up guys again. Lesson learned. Without ceremony, I left his building and headed back to my dorm room. I wasn't hungry anymore.

8

Despite my rush to get away from Sean's apartment, I walked slowly back to the south dorms. There were several paths I could take around the campus, and for some reason, I chose one I hadn't taken before—the fraternity and sorority row. At least a dozen of old manor-like houses stretched through the long street, all of them looking a little creepy and even haunted in the cover of the night.

I couldn't help but look around, not only on the lookout for random ghosts, but also for Brotherhood members and other supernaturals. Like Lenora had warned me, New Orleans was full of them, and not all of them had good intentions. I would wager that most of them didn't.

As I walked by the houses, I could see a handful of them had parties. Loud music and a crowd of students spilled from the buildings, and many students held red plastic cups.

A girl stumbled out of one of the houses, carrying her

red cup with her. She tripped on the front steps, almost kissed the ground, but didn't lose the grip on her cup. In fact, when she regained her footing, she tipped the cup up and drank the rest of whatever that was. Then she threw the cup to the side and staggered down the walkway to the sideway, moving her arms as if she was underwater to keep balance.

This girl was way too drunk. She would either fall over and crack her skull or—

A shadow moved behind a thick tree in the house's front yard. My steps faltered as I saw a guy in a long black coat approach the girl. He looked like a predator going for its prey. He reached for her and she didn't even object when he hooked her arm on his and he guided her to the side of the house.

I watched, my stomach sinking. She had gone so willingly, he must have been a friend. Right? But she was too drunk to tell, right? And if he was a friend, why was he taking her to the alley between the houses, where it was even darker and quieter?

It didn't sit well with me.

Sighing, I slipped my hand inside my purse, closed my fist around my crystal—just in case I need to shoot sparks at this guy's feet to run him off—and followed them.

I turned the alley and stopped short, my breath stuck in my throat.

The guy wasn't just a guy.

He pushed the drunk girl against the wall and leaned over her, baring his fangs.

A vampire.

I clutched the crystal tighter and channeled my magic. I didn't know what damage I could do against a vampire, but I could try to distract him so that the girl could get away.

Finally, the girl woke up from her stupor and screamed, but the vampire covered her mouth with his hand, muffling it. I strode into the alley.

From the other side, two figures marched toward the vampire. The vamp noticed their presence and turned to the newcomers, letting the girl go. She screamed and ran, almost losing her balance and falling again. I reached for her and helped her run for a few steps.

But I didn't go with her. Instead, I stayed practically frozen in my spot as I stared at the scene before my eyes. Two women with long black swords emanating a green shine stood in front of the vampire.

Blackthorn Demon Hunters.

I had read a little bit about them. They were somewhat like the Brotherhood of Purity, though the Brotherhood cared more about hunting witches, especially Lightgrove and Darkmist ones, while the Blackthorn Demon Hunters went after all supernaturals.

I should run, I should hide, but I couldn't strip my eyes from the badass women who brandished their swords with clear expertise and in less than a minute had disposed of the vampire.

His body fell on the ground with a heavy thud.

And the two demon hunters locked their eyes on me.

Oh, shit.

Flight, fight, or freeze. I was caught between the three of them.

"Don't worry, we won't harm you," one of the hunters said, lowering her hands. The shine of the black blade glinted off her dark red hair before the sword disappeared into thin air.

Swallowing my fear, I took a large step back. "That's what they all say."

"We're not what you think," the blonde one said. She showed me her hands just as her sword magically faded away. "You've probably heard stories that Blackthorn Demon Hunters hunt all supernaturals, regardless of what they are."

True. Everyone had heard that. "We're not what you think," I repeated. "Another rehearsed line."

"It's true," the red haired one said. "Look, we're under new leadership. We know not all supernaturals are evil."

I frowned.

"Are you one of the Lightgrove witches?" the blonde asked. "We're here to meet with your coven. Peacefully."

"We came to explain the changes and our goal to protect humans only from supernaturals who try to harm them. We also protect good supernaturals from evil ones." The red hair one gestured to herself, before pointing to the blonde hunter. "I'm Doreen, and this is Norah."

Norah waved her hand at me. "Nice to meet you."

Several questions tugged at my mind. "Hm, if you're here to meet with the Lightgrove witches, how come you're here, at Towland?"

"Our audience was postponed until Saturday," Doreen said. "In the meantime, we're trying to be useful."

"We saw you were going to save that girl from the vampire," Norah said. She toed the vampire's body and my stomach revolved. "Very brave."

"And also stupid," I muttered. "I'm not that powerful." Probably shouldn't have told them that. If they were lying, now they could easily overtake me. "I'm not one of the Lightgrove witches."

Not yet, at least. If I passed their test.

"Oh. You seemed like one," Doreen said.

All right. This was getting awkward. "Um, I should go."

"Of course." Norah waved me off. "You go ahead and we'll take care of the body."

"Be careful," Doreen said. "We've been here less than two days and already have had too many run-ins with supernaturals trying to harm humans."

I nodded, as I had been learning that myself. Without another word, I turned and left the alley. Once I was back on the sidewalk leading toward campus, something in me tightened and I ran.

I ran back to my dorm, suddenly overcome by all that had been happening these past few days—first the Brotherhood, now a vampire and two demon hunters. And everyone around me told me to be careful because of the supernaturals in New Orleans.

It seemed I hadn't chosen the best city to move to.

9

Towland was busy for a Thursday evening, not with students going to classes, but with students walking around, getting ready for parties, or leaving to go party downtown.

Krissa was one of the many going to the French Quarter, and I was able to get a ride with her. She teased me during the twenty-minute drive, asking me which bar I was going to, who I was sneaking around with. If only ... I tuned her out and thought about last night—Sean and the Blackthorn Demon Hunters I had encountered.

It had taken me a long time to fall asleep last night, because my mind kept going back to not only Sean and his sour mood, and how that had affected me, but also the fact that there were two demon hunters on campus, hunting down vampires and other supernaturals—evil ones, they had said. They didn't kill all supernaturals anymore. Could that be true? I wanted to believe it. After all, they had let me go, but that could have been a trick. But why would they trick me? If they hunted anyone, I would be dead already.

I pushed those thoughts out of my head when Krissa drove her beat-up Corolla into the parking garage off North Rampart Street. From there, I walked three blocks to Bourbon Street. At this time of the evening, the place was alive, milling with people, colors, scents, and sounds. Bright lights cast an eerie shine on the street; red, orange, green, and blue building walls added to the lively scenery; and a jazz group, dressed in 1920s clothing, played in the middle of the street, gathering a huge crowd around them, and filling the place with smooth, sassy songs. The air smelled of beignets, whiskey, and sweet perfume.

I smiled, infected by the place.

But my smile faded as I remembered the couple of warnings I had received lately and the sighting of the Brotherhood of Purity, a vampire, and two demon hunters. Though I knew the supernatural population was like a half percent that of the human population, if that much, it seemed they liked to flock close together—and New Orleans was a hotspot.

On Bourbon Street, I weaved through the crowd for another two blocks until I entered an alleyway and halted before the Midnight Cauldron. It would have been an odd name if this weren't the French Quarter, where dozens of voodoo shops were located. Some were posers to attract tourists, but a few were the real thing, and the Midnight Cauldron was famous among my kind.

There was no sign or bright light indicating the shop was open, but I turned the door's knob and pushed. As I'd expected, the witch doctor was behind the counter of the overstuffed place.

"Evening, child," said Khalisa, the witch doctor. As usual, her lips were painted black and her hair was threaded into thick dreadlocks. Her dark skin shone under the dim light, hiding the freckles spread over her cheeks and nose. Her clothes reminded me of a costume from an old pirate movie, with ragged skirts, a tight bodice, and too much cleavage.

"I brought a list of items I'll need." I handed her the piece of paper where I had written the ingredients for the spells and potions I would use tomorrow night.

She took it from me without ceremony. "Lumin, chamomile, rosemary, caraway, thyme, damiana, Spanish moss, basil, euphrasia, boswelia thurifera, hawthorn berry, anise, garlic cloves, bloodstone powder, amethyst, salt, and black candles. Based on the quantity of each item and their use, I can guess you plan to chase every ghost in this city and send them away."

I grimaced. "Something like that."

Her dark eyes bored into mine. "You aren't that foolish." When I first met her two months ago, Khalisa had been unfriendly, in a crazed-like manner. If she hadn't come with a recommendation from my mother's friends, I wouldn't have lasted ten seconds inside her shop. With time, I got used to her craziness and sharp mind. I think that, in her way, she had warmed up to me. Not to the point of sweet smiles and hugs and nice words, but to the point of warnings and caution.

The truth was, Khalisa hadn't been born a witch

doctor. She was a witch from the Wildthorn coven. For some reason I didn't know, she had left the coven long ago and learned voodoo magic, thus becoming a witch doctor. With her dark sense of humor, she thought it was amusing to open a real voodoo shop in the French Quarter, of all places.

I sighed. "I have no choice."

"And why is that, child?"

"It's my duty. Every witch helps a ghost to cross, if she can. And Friday the Thirteenth is a big night for that. I have to go to St. Louis cemetery, the City Park, the Saenger Theatre, Hotel Monteleone, a random abandoned mansion in the Garden District, a—"

"What mansion?" She squinted at me, the crazed glint always there.

"I don't know. Some random mansion. I haven't been in this city long. I'll have to look for it tomorrow."

"Do you have a specific address?"

"Yes." I told her the address and her eyes widened. "What?"

"A girl and a young man died there last year on Halloween night."

I gaped. "What?"

"The mansion is said to be haunted, and they went there with another young man on a dare. The mansion is indeed haunted, and the ghosts, trying to escape to this world, killed them."

I gasped. No, it couldn't be. "Do you know the names of the victims?"

She thought for a second before turning her back to

me and reaching under the counter. She pulled out a book with a worn leather cover. She opened it, revealing several newspaper and magazine articles.

"I collect the articles when something strikes me as magical or supernatural." It was ordered by date and soon she found it. "Here it is. Lizzie Flaherty and Doug Marks." She turned the book to me and I leaned over it.

Flaherty. Holy shit, it was Sean's sister.

The article spread over an entire page of the newspaper and pictures of Lizzie and Doug took up the top right corner. She looked like her brother, with bright eyes and dark hair.

The article told the story of how Doug and Sean had gone to the haunted mansion on Halloween night, and after finding out about it, Lizzie followed them. Then, things got complicated. Sean told the police that they knew the place wasn't really haunted, that it was a local story, but still they were fine, having fun, until the temperature dropped, lights that shouldn't have been connected to the main line flickered, and the shadows grew. He said people came out of nowhere, and killed his sister and his best friend. He was able to run from the house before they got a hold of him and call 911. When the police got there, they didn't find anyone other than Sean, and the mangled bodies of Lizzie and Doug. Sean was taken in, and after a long interrogation, followed by a psychological evaluation, which determined he was in shock, they let him go. The killers were never found.

Holy shit.

Temperature drop? Lights flickering? Shadows growing? The mansion was definitely haunted, and ghosts had killed Lizzie and Doug. Poor Sean. Of course he couldn't explain what he saw. Of course everyone would discard his story as shock. No wonder he was so lonely.

"I need to avenge these people," I said.

"You'd have to be mad to go in there, child," the witch doctor said, losing her grin. "That place is the hottest ghost point in this entire city. It will be even worse on a Friday the Thirteenth night."

I closed the book. "I know, but it's my job."

Shaking her head, she put the book away. "Tomorrow is a full moon. You know what that means, right?"

I nodded. The moon was powerful and influenced the lives of all paranormal creatures—witches, ghosts, werewolves, etc. Supposedly, we all became more powerful. Which meant the ghosts would be even worse to deal with. "I'll have to find a way to handle it," I said, hoping my voice didn't betray the nervousness and the fear brewing in me.

"All right, child. I can see I won't persuade you to give up this idea." The witch doctor walked around the counter and to a tall shelf in a corner. She crouched down, opened a drawer, and withdrew a wooden box from inside it. She returned to where I was standing and halted before me. "Then you should have this." She opened the box lid. A thin leather necklace with a tiny, dirty bone for a pendant rested in white velvet.

It looked evil. I scrunched my nose. "What is it for?"

"This bone is said to be from a powerful witch," she said, and I wondered if she knew about the founder of the Lightgrove coven. As if reading my mind, she continued.

"Not Arianna's. Nobody knows where she was buried. Besides, she was pure ashes after her death. No bones. But it's said to be Brita's, one of her mentors and best friends."

I gasped. It couldn't be. Brita had been dead for almost as long as Arianna had. Over six hundred years ago. How and when had someone found her bones?

There was no denying the power coming from it from the moment the witch doctor opened the box. I reached for the necklace and brushed my fingertip against the bone. A jolt of magic surged into my veins, startling me and making me jump back.

"Whoa."

The witch doctor grinned—a totally crazed expression. "Yes. It has more power than your crystals. You can draw from it if needed."

Wow. Me with a fraction of Brita's powers? That would be amazing, surreal, like a dream come true. I gulped. "But ... it probably cost a lot and I don't have this kind of money."

She deposited the box on the counter and took the necklace in her hands. "You don't need to pay me if I lend this to you. Give it back to me once your task is complete."

"A-are you sure?"

Nodding, she walked behind me and clasped the necklace around my neck. I gasped again as the magic flowed into me. It cooled me, it warmed me, it swirled inside me, and it made me feel invincible.

"There, child. Now you have a chance against that mansion," the witch doctor said.

I glanced at the bone hanging from my neck. "Thank you."

She marched back behind the counter. "I'll work on your list. Come back tomorrow morning and I'll have everything ready for you."

I tucked the necklace under my thin sweater. "All right. Thanks again."

The witch doctor waved me off as if I was the most boring thing she had ever seen, and I smiled.

10

AFTER I EXITED THE MIDNIGHT CAULDRON, I HEADED TO ST. Louis Cathedral. I wasn't the praying type, but the last ingredient I needed was holy water and there was no better place to get some. I could have chosen a smaller church or chapel, but usually St. Louis was full of tourists, even on a Friday night. It would be easier to blend in.

I had never been to the cathedral, and once I stepped inside, I halted, sucking in a long breath. It was magnificent, with a tall, arched ceiling painted with several depictions of Jesus. Galleries, colored glass windows, chandeliers, flags, a beautiful altar, and many tourists. Perfect.

With the crowd, I approached one of the two statues of angels holding bowls. Bowls that were filled with holy water. I fished the small vial from inside my pocket and held it in my hand.

When it was my turn, I whispered under my breath, *"Delabor."*

The lady behind me tripped on her foot and fell on her knees. Several people turned to help her, giving me my chance. I dipped my fingertips in the water and let the vial fill. Pressing it down, the vial immersed and, three seconds later, I picked it up with my thumb and forefinger. I closed my hand around it and moved on, while everyone was still worried about the lady who couldn't explain how she had fallen.

I took a few steps into the main aisle and stopped. Was it worth it to pray and ask for help? I shook my head, feeling silly. My kind prayed to other gods and goddesses.

As I turned to leave, I spotted someone sitting in the last pew on the left, under the gallery and away from the others. His elbows were propped on his knees and his head was low. Though I couldn't see his face, the black hoodie and the red bracelet on his wrist told me I knew this guy.

A rush of dread and concern fleeted through me. I wanted to approach him, but after last evening, I wasn't sure I should. I had thought about him a lot last night. About how disturbed and lost he was, and how I really wanted to help him. Which was crazy. Why was I torturing myself like that?

Convinced I would regret my decision, I sat on the bench and scooted closer to him, but not too close.

Sean lifted his head, leaned back into the bench, and stared at me with wide eyes. "What are you doing here?" The bruises on his face were now black.

"I could ask you the same thing," I said, trying to sound casual. "You don't look like the praying type."

One corner of his lips quirked up—my heart sped up—and his gaze traveled over me. "With that hair, piercing, tattoo, and all, I would think the same of you."

I shrugged. "What? Just because my style is a little different, I'm supposed to be a faithless bad girl? A troublemaker?"

Sean returned his eyes to mine. "Well, I like your style."

I felt a little blush creeping into my cheeks. As if realizing he had said something he shouldn't, he turned his gaze to the altar.

Damn it. The guy couldn't say things like that and then leave me hanging. And why the hell was I thinking about that? The guy was damaged, broken, depressed. And he was rude to me yesterday. As much as I wanted, flirting with him was not right. Not until I helped him. Because I did want to help him. In fact, I wanted to tell him I was going to the mansion tomorrow night, and I would avenge his sister and his best friend. Hopefully, knowing they were resting in peace, Sean would be able to move on.

However, if I tried to say anything about that right now, I would probably scar him more.

I swallowed hard. "Are you okay?"

Slowly, Sean looked at me again. "I don't know. I'm alive, I'm healthy, but ..." He pressed his mouth tight.

I reached to him and clasped his hand in mine. "What?"

He stared at our hands for a moment. "I come here every time I don't feel okay. Every time I feel lost. Every time I feel like I want to break everything, everyone. I was never the praying type, as you phrased it, but my sister was. She came here for Mass at least twice a month, and she always said that, since I didn't pray, she prayed for me." My heart tugged and I squeezed his hand. "This weekend she would have turned nineteen. She died last October."

I know. I wanted to tell him. I mean, a lot of people on campus knew about it. Maybe I could say I had heard from someone. But then he would think I was prying into his life. No, no. I would let him open up. Little by little.

"I'm sorry," I whispered.

"Me too," he whispered back.

"Want to talk about it?" I asked, knowing the answer.

He shook his head. "Not really. I don't like thinking about it, much less talking." I caressed his hand, and my thumb touched the macramé bracelet on his wrist. A small smile appeared on his handsome face, illuminating his blue eyes. "My sister made that for me on my birthday a few years ago. She had one too. She said it was our thing."

"It seems you two had a special bond."

He nodded. "She was sixteen months younger than me, and we were best friends since she was born." He pulled his hand away from mine and leaned to the front again, his elbows on his knees. "I'm ... I'm sorry about yesterday." He sighed. "You were trying to help me and I was a jerk. I'm really sorry."

I hadn't really expected an apology. "It's okay."

"No. It's not." He pressed his lips together before proceeding. "I went to the bar to watch the game and grab a bite. I was all quiet on my own until a guy recognized me and started talking about the night my sister and my best friend died, saying I was a nut job. I tried to ignore him, but he started shoving me and I lost it." He went quiet.

Biting my lip, I sat back in the pew, unsure what to do. If I was going to help him, baby steps were the way to go. Pushing him right now would send him running. In silence, I stayed beside Sean for ten minutes, hoping he would come to recognize me as an anchor of some sort. Only time would tell.

I reached over and patted him on the back. He went rigid with my touch, but didn't pull away. Finally, I stood and walked out of the cathedral, thinking I had to be demented to want a damaged guy like Sean to find an anchor in me. What if he was truly lost and insane? What if he had a breakdown and dragged me with him?

I pushed those thoughts out of my mind. I would worry about him and his situation after Friday the Thirteenth. Right now, I had to prepare myself for the day to come.

BEING IN THE FRENCH QUARTER MADE ME INCREDIBLY nervous now, but I decided I couldn't stop living just because there were more things out there than I could see.

So after walking out of the cathedral, I went to the Café Du Monde, where I ordered a box of beignets to go. When I was little, beignets weren't the most common sweet we ate. In fact, every time we ate beignets, it was for a special occasion like a birthday, a graduation, or another celebration. It was not that beignets were that expensive, it was that my mother wasn't a great cook and she refused to buy them that often.

But now, living here in New Orleans, I could splurge.

It was dark when I exited Café Du Monde and called an Uber. While waiting, I glanced around the street, taking in the tourists, the costumes, the music, the lights, the scent of bourbon, cigar, and sweet perfume. My gaze halted at a shop across the street.

The Dark Veil.

The building was painted black, the lettering in silver, and the window covered most of the side of the shop. For some reason, I walked closer and spied in the window.

A cold feeling rolled over my shoulders and down my spine.

The glass door opened and a woman in a black gown stepped out. Her dark eyes met mine before she moved on. But in that brief second she had looked at me, I felt it. She was a supernatural.

I turned my attention back to the window—the place was crowded with a lot of customers, and I knew they were all supernaturals. Their races were all on the tip of my tongue ... vampire, werewolf, witch, even a succubus.

A gasp rose to my throat and I took a large step back from that window. How could I have known they were all supernaturals? How could I have guessed what they were? I didn't have that kind of magic.

I touched the bone pendant resting against my collarbone. It was the magic in it. It had to be. The pendant was so powerful, I could now at least sense the supernaturals, even if I couldn't really understand it.

A man opened the shop's door and went in—another supernatural, but something darker.

A demon?

My phone dinged, indicating my Uber was here.

I whirled on my heels and dashed to the car, suddenly fearful of ever stepping foot in the French Quarter again.

11

THE FIRST THING I DID ON THE MORNING OF FRIDAY THE Thirteenth was ditch my classes for the day and stop by the Midnight Cauldron to pick up my ingredients. The second thing was to make sure Krissa wasn't in our room (she had stayed at her hookup's apartment apparently), lock the door, and prepare the potions.

If I had had more time, I would have been able to make some powerful potions, but with little warning, these ones would have to do. Hopefully, the bone necklace's magic would compensate for it.

I fished four small cauldrons from under my bed, conjured a light in the middle of my room, and mixed the ingredients. While the potions brewed, I did my homework, got ahead on a project, ate, took a shower, and put on my mission clothes: black leggings, a black long-sleeved tee, a black leather jacket, and black combat boots. I pulled my hair up in a ponytail and applied my mascara and eyeliner.

In the evening, the quantity of voices and footsteps ringing from behind my door increased. Everyone was getting ready for the parties—the one on campus and the others around the city.

At some point, Krissa came back to change. I had already stashed everything under my bed and recast the invisibility spell. She dressed in a skimpy nurse outfit and stood in front of our only full-length mirror behind the bathroom door.

"I look great, don't I?" She whirled around, proud of looking naughty.

I smiled, not because I agreed, but because she amused me. "Yup."

She stared at me through the mirror. "And what are you supposed to be? That chick from that vampire and werewolf movie?"

I shook my head. "That's Selene from *Underworld*. And no. I dressed up, but no costume."

"You're no fun." She picked up her tiny purse. "Well, don't wait up for me. I probably won't come back tonight. Again." She winked before leaving the room.

I waited a good fifteen minutes before dragging my things from under my bed again. I hid all the vials in a black utility belt, placed a dagger with them, made sure I had the bone necklace, and left my room.

Opposite to the sea of students leaving the building, I went up to the fourth floor. The door to room 408 was closed, and there was no light coming from under it. A couple of girls walked by, and after making sure they were gone and there wasn't anyone else coming, I rested my ear to the door and listened for signs of anyone inside. Too quiet.

Voices came from the end of the hallway, and I pushed away from the door. I knelt down and pretended to fix my boots. The girls, all dressed up for the party, didn't even see me as they walked by. They rushed down the stairs and I returned my attention to the room.

I touched the cold metal knob. "*Aperi.*" The lock made a click sound, and I twisted the knob, pushing the door open.

The room was much messier than Krissa's and mine, and much pinker. And purple. I stepped in and a force pushed me back.

What the ...?

The power filled the room, as if declaring ownership. Oh no. I clutched the bone in my hand and channeled my power. My veins filled with magic, a wave of bliss and power, a rush that made me feel strong and right.

I tried entering the room again. The ghost pushed me back, but this time, it was no match for the magic flowing in me. I stopped in the middle of the room and called it forth. "*Apparet.*"

White smoke appeared in front of me, slowly morphing into a human shape. Legs, a fluffy dress that came down to her knees, thin waist, arms, hair separated into two braids, and a fuzzy face.

A girl. The ghost was a girl.

I called on the magic, focusing on her face, wanting it to be clear.

Her white eyes widened, and the hazy expression on

her face was of pure terror. She reached for me and opened her mouth, but nothing came out.

"What is it?" I asked. "You want to tell me something?"

She nodded. She opencd her mouth again, looking desperate to say something.

"*Claritas*," I said, invoking magic to help her.

"You," she croaked, her voice raspy. She touched her throat and tried again. "You can't—"

She vanished.

My mouth fell open and I looked around. What the hell? Even her power, her force was gone. I couldn't feel her anywhere. I looked out the window, trying to get a reading if she was out there, just out of reach, but I didn't feel or see anything.

Focusing on my magic, I called her again. "*Apparet.*" I tried it a couple more times, without success.

My phone dinged and I fished it out of my jacket pocket. The reminder I had put in had beeped. It was time to go. It pained me to leave the ghost of this girl without resolution, but I had to go if I didn't want to fail the light witches' test without even trying.

***

KNOWING THE MANSION WOULD BE A BIGGER CHALLENGE, I headed to some of the other spots first. Some were easy peasy, just the normal ghost hunting job. Closing the cuts was a bit harder, but nothing that needed too much power or complicated spells—not with the bone pendant. The City Park, the Hotel Monteleone, the Saenger Theatre, and the St. Louis Cemetery required a bit more time—especially to hide from tourists and guests—and a couple of potions.

From outside, the mansion didn't look haunted, just old and uncared for. I stood on the sidewalk, outside the tall, rusty gates, and looked at the place. Three stories with a turret on the right corner, a large front porch, and half a dozen broken stairs to the double front door. The once-white paint was graying and peeling; the roof was dirty and had several broken spots. Some of the windows had hanging shutters or shattered glass.

With magic, I pushed open the gate and walked up to the porch. The power emanating from inside only grew with each step I took.

I swallowed my fear, climbed up the steps, and reached for the knob. I peeked inside, afraid the ghosts would be right there and would overwhelm me before I had a chance to get started. The light coming from the full moon seeped through the windows and illuminated the interior. A large, square foyer extended in front of me, a once beautiful crystal chandelier hung precariously from the ceiling, and double staircases extended from each side of the room, leading up to a landing upstairs. Under the staircase, an archway led to the rest of the house.

Cautious, I stepped inside. It was cold in here and the power was even stronger, but not as strong as if the cut in the veil were open. I frowned. Why wasn't the cut open yet? I pulled my phone from my jacket pocket and checked the time. One hour to midnight. Oh crap. What if I had missed the window? What if the veil had already opened, let out a bunch of ghosts, and now was closed once again? Shit. Here was where I was supposed to prove myself to the light witches. How was I supposed to do that if the cut was gone?

Wait, no. The cuts would still be open if not forced closed. It was true for the others, and this one wouldn't be any different. The cut here hadn't opened yet, and I couldn't draw a circle and start the spell until it did.

I held my breath as a ghost of an old man walked across the upstairs landing, emerging from one wall and disappearing into the other.

I turned to close the door, before a ghost noticed something was out of order, when someone came barreling inside, bumping into me and almost making me yelp and fall. I pressed a hand over my mouth and the person held my elbow, keeping me up.

"Sorry."

I gasped, recognizing that voice. I grabbed his biceps and pulled him to a thin strip of moonlight. No. No. No.

"What are you doing here?" I whispered, wanting to scream at him.

Sean looked at me as if I was crazy. "What are *you* doing here?"

"Shhh." I tried pushing him back out the door, but he was much bigger than me and didn't budge. "You have to go. Now."

"No. You have to go. I won't leave if you don't leave with me." He reached for me and held my hand, a gentle touch that was opposite of the terror illustrating his face. "Please, let's go. You have no idea the bad things that can happen here." He tugged my arm. "Come on."

"Sean," I whispered. "I can't go. But you have to."

Nodding, he let go of my hand and I exhaled a relieved breath. He would leave and I would be able to work without interference.

Instead, Sean grabbed me around the middle and hoisted me over his shoulder. His arm wound around my thighs, just below my butt, and he ran out of the mansion. I had to bite my tongue so I wouldn't yell for him to let me go.

I jerked on his grasp. "Put me down," I demanded, maintaining a low voice.

He raced down the front porch's stairs. I jolted on his shoulder, kicking my legs and punching his back. He didn't even flinch.

Finally, in front of the gates, he set me down. "There."

I straightened my jacket. "Why did you do that?"

"Because!" he yelled, clenching his fists.

"Don't raise your voice." I sighed. "Sean, please, leave and don't come back."

I stepped away from him, but he wrapped his hand around my wrist and yanked me back. "Where the hell do you think you're going?"

I stared at him, not one bit affected by his raging glare. "Please, please, please, release me and go away."

He pulled me closer. "Hazel, this place is ..." He pressed his mouth shut and shook his head.

I relaxed a bit. "This place is evil. I know. I read about what happened during Halloween last year, but I would like you to tell me about it." He shook his head. I turned to him and, with my free hand, touched his arm. "Please, Sean, tell me. I swear I'll believe you."

He snorted, a sound full of sarcasm. "Not even I believe what my own eyes saw. Why would you?"

"Try me."

He stared at me, those bright blue eyes softening. He must have seen something in me, because he sighed and said, "I ... Doug and I had always heard about the haunted places in New Orleans and we always said we should visit them during Halloween. Last year, we finally did it. We chose this house because it's said to be the worst of the haunted places. Deep down, we thought it was all stories for the tourists. I never thought ..." He paused and looked up at the full moon. "I never thought it could be real. At least, I think it was real. Psychiatrists say I had a break-down and everything was my imagination. At some point, I think I believed them. I believed I was hallucinating." He glanced back at the house. "However, here we are, and I can't shake the feeling that it was real."

"What was real?"

He faced me again, his eyes frightened. "Ghosts. So many ghosts. And they were corporeal, most of them. They grabbed us, they played with us, they tortured us. Finally, I was able to break free, and I was about to help Lizzie and Doug, but the ghosts killed them. Right in front of me. I saw the light go out in their eyes. I saw their bodies slump. The ghosts turned to me, and I ran." He closed his eyes. "I ran like a coward."

"No, Sean. You're not a coward." I pulled him into a

tight embrace. He was rigid at first, and then he melted into me. His arms snaked around me, pulling me close. "Ghosts are vengeful and evil. Most of the ones that stay in this world are. There wasn't much you could have done."

He lifted his head to look at me, a big V between his brows. "I just told you I saw ghosts, and you aren't telling me I must have imagined things."

I could lie. I could say he was imagining things. But maybe he was here at this exact moment for a reason. Maybe he was supposed to find out about ghosts and the other world so he could move on.

"Because you didn't. Ghosts are real. I can see them."

His eyes went wide. "W-what?"

What the hell? I was going all the way now. "I'm a witch, Sean. In my spare time, I help ghosts cross over to the other world."

Suspicion spread through his face and he stepped back from me. "Is this a joke?"

I sighed, extending my hand between us. I channeled my power and whispered, "*Lux.*" A ball of light danced at the end of my fingertips. Sean retreated another step. "There are several kinds of witches. I'm a light witch."

He stared at the magic bolt, mesmerized. "If there are light witches, then ..."

"There are also dark witches. Bad witches. And there are witch hunters too, the Brotherhood of Purity. They hunt light and dark witches, since, to them, we're all witches, which means we're all evil."

He locked his eyes on mine. "Why are you telling me all this?"

I closed my hand and the light vanished. "Because I'm here to do my job, Sean. Soon, somewhere inside the house, a cut will open in the veil between our worlds and more ghosts will come out. I need to close the veil and send the ghosts back. I'll avenge your sister and your friend, and hopefully you'll feel better after that. But right now, I need you to stay away from the house, okay?"

He reached for me. "Wait, no—"

I stepped out of his grasp. "Stay safe."

With a small smile, I turned around and walked back to the house.

12

I ENTERED THE MANSION FEELING BOTH RELIEVED AND nervous. Relieved that Sean had stayed outside, and nervous because it was eleven thirty and there still was no sign of the cut. It should open any time now.

I leaned on the door, intent on closing it without a sound, when it was pushed back on me. Sean barged in again.

"What are you doing here?" I whispered.

"I can't let you do this alone," he whispered back.

"Sean. I have magic. I have potions. You don't have any kind of weapon against them. I can't think about protecting you while I'm busy casting spells to close the veil."

A muscle in his jaw popped. "You don't have to worry about me. I'll be fine."

I shook my head and pushed him back. "No. Please, Sean, leave. I'll feel better."

He held my hands in his and looked into my eyes. "I

lost someone special to me here. I won't let it happen again."

My heart squeezed. I wanted to ask him what he meant by that, whether he wouldn't let another person die here, or if I was someone special to him. I wanted to revel in his words and daydream about the meaning. But hell, this was not the time!

"I want *you* to be safe." I yanked my hands from him and sent a wave of air over him. It pushed him back to the door. But, before he could cross the threshold, the door closed itself.

Sean bumped into it. "Ouch."

My blood chilled. I turned around. The ghost of an old woman was on the right side of the staircase, and she had a wicked grin on her twisted face.

Damn it. I put myself between Sean and her as she let out a screech and floated toward us. I channeled the magic from the necklace and sent a wave of energy to her, slowing her down. Meanwhile, I reached inside my utility belt and grabbed the pouch with the red powder.

Her white fingers inched closer. I threw the powder at her and chanted, "*Liberi.*"

The ghost exploded into white smoke.

"Whoa," Sean muttered from behind me.

"Come on." I grabbed his hand and pulled him under the staircase. "Her scream might have alerted others that there's someone in the house."

We crossed the archway into a huge living room. A door on the left caught my attention. I opened it and, after noticing it was a small closet, pushed Sean in and joined him. I closed the door and cast a light bolt in my palm to illuminate the cramped space. Not wasting time, I picked the pouch of salt from my belt and formed a small circle around us.

"Is that salt?" Sean asked.

I nodded. "Stay in the circle." He stepped in and his chest brushed with mine. He was hard and tall and wide. I felt myself blushing, which was ridiculous. How could I feel like this in such a dire situation?

"Won't they find us here?" Sean asked.

"I'm channeling our energy. The salt helps. Hopefully, they won't notice us yet." I kept my right arm extended to the side so the light illuminated everything.

Sean placed his hand on my forearm and slid his palm under my hand. Even through two layers of fabric, I could feel the warmth of his touch. I shivered.

He closed my hand, putting out the light. "Now they can't find us because of the brightness," he whispered.

"Right." My heart raced. He hadn't let go of my hand yet.

"Aren't you afraid?"

I raised my head to glance at him, wishing the light was still lit so I could stare at his beautiful blue eyes, but at the same time, I was glad we were in the dark or I wouldn't be this brave.

"A little. I'm used to this kind of thing, just not on this scale."

His fingertips traced my cheek and I inhaled sharply. "The way you just marched in this house and confronted that ghost, it was badass."

I chuckled. "I think I like that."

His breath teased my cheek and I gasped. I had no idea his face was that close to mine. Acting on the rush of desire running inside me, I tilted my head back and lifted on my tiptoes—

A surge of power rushed through me, sending me to my knees.

Sean clasped my elbows and pulled me up. "What happened?"

"The cut. It must be opening."

I reached for the door and Sean pulled me back. "What are you doing?"

"Hiding was never part of the plan. I need to do something."

He squeezed my hand. "Please, be careful."

I smiled, even though he couldn't see it. "I'll try."

Slowly, I opened the closet door and spied out.

The living room was huge. High ceiling, tall windows, balconies from the second and third floor, another big crystal chandelier, scratched wooden floors, and some scattered furniture—a broken side table, a ripped couch, a tipped bookshelf.

And right beside the chandelier, sparks came to life. The cut in the making.

After looking side-to-side and making sure no ghosts were out there, I raced to the center of the room and started drawing a circle under the cut. From the corner of my eye, I saw Sean spying from inside the closet, his head darting side-to-side, looking for ghosts.

Apparently, he didn't see the one that came from under

the floor and knocked me aside before I could close the circle.

"Hazel!" Sean rushed to me.

I groaned as I landed on my side. The ghost, a young woman with empty eyes and bared teeth, hovered over me. I raised my hand and threw a little red powder at her. "*Liberi*," I said. She burst into smoke.

Sean extended his hand to me and helped me up. "If you give me some of that powder and I say those same words, will it work too?"

I wiped my hands on my pants. "I'm not sure." The shrill of more ghosts filled the air. "That sounded like a lot. We need to hide and have the advantage again."

We started for the closet, but another ghost appeared in our way. The same girl from the dorm. Now I recognized her dress. She was dressed like Dorothy from the *Wizard of Oz*.

"Come with me," she said, beckoning us to follow.

"You can talk now," I said. She nodded. "Why should we trust you?"

She pointed to Sean. "Ask him."

I turned to Sean and he was frozen by my side, pale as the ghost in front of us. "Sean, what's the matter?"

He blinked. "Lizzie. Is that really you?"

Oh. *Oh!*

She smiled. "Yes." The shrieks of ghosts reverberated again. "Come on. Now."

We followed her to a hallway, and then into what looked like an abandoned office. I closed the door and rested against it.

Sean stared at his sister. "H-how?"

She looked at me instead. "There's a Darkmist witch here. She was here last Halloween too. She comes back often, actually. She is the one opening the cut and ordering ghosts out. She takes them with her."

Sean paled. "There was a witch here that night?" Lizzie nodded at him. "I didn't see her."

"When I saw her, it was too late," Lizzie said.

"So, that's what you were trying to tell me before? About the dark witch?" I asked and she nodded again. "Why does she take the ghosts?"

She shrugged. "I can only go to limited locations. Here, my old dorm, which is where you saw me earlier, some of my old classrooms, my parents' house."

"So you couldn't follow her," I said.

She shook her head. "No. I know though that I still haven't passed to the other side because of her. She caused my death, and now she'll take me with her once the cut closes again."

"Oh no, she won't," Sean barked. His fists were clenched, his nostrils flared.

Lizzie smiled. "Always protective."

His shoulders sagged. "I didn't protect you."

She hovered to him, and I could see her becoming corporeal. She held his hands. "What happened isn't your fault. *We* came here, *we* thought it was a joke, and *we* played with things much more powerful than us. I'm just glad you made it out."

He embraced her tightly. "I wish you had made it out

too." Eyes wide, he pulled back and looked at me. "Can you bring her back?"

A pang ran through my heart. "No, Sean. There's no spell for that, and even if there were, I'm not powerful enough."

Sean frowned. "Lizzie, how about Doug?"

Her expression fell. "He was taken by the dark witch a long time ago. I never saw him again."

"You have no idea what happened to him?" Sean asked.

"My guess is that he's still in this world, like me, but working for the dark witch. If she is as bad as she seems, I'm glad I wasn't taken yet."

"You won't be taken." Sean glanced at me. "Right?"

Lizzie looked at me too. "You don't know me and I have no right to ask you for a favor, but please stop this witch and help me find peace."

Before I had the pressure of failing and being a disgrace to my mother, to my family. Now Lizzie was asking me to save her, and Sean would expect the same. The pressure increased.

I gulped. "I'll do my best."

13

THE THREE OF US INCHED BACK TO THE LIVING ROOM. THE cut was growing, but not quite open yet. I glanced up and saw the dark witch on the balcony of the second floor, her arms open as if trying to embrace the cut. Her power was overwhelming. For a moment, I wondered how she didn't sense me here, but with such strong magic and focused on the cut, she wouldn't notice me sneaking in.

Her face wasn't pretty, but her features were strong and her eyes huge, shining with darkness—like most dark witches. Or so I was told. I had encountered only one other dark witch. I didn't remember much. Only that my mother, my sister, and I were visiting my grandmother and a dark witch got in our way while we were out. She almost killed my grandmother, who had come to help us, but then hunters arrived and we vanished before they could get us too.

I leaned into Sean and whispered into his ear, "Close

the circle." I put a piece of white chalk made of pearl powder in his hand.

He grabbed my arms, holding me in place, and turned his head toward mine. "What are you going to do?"

"I'll stop the dark witch."

"But—"

"I have to. It's the only way to free your sister."

He stared into my eyes, concern written all over his handsome features. "Kick her ass."

I smiled. "Thanks for the vote of confidence."

Sean leaned into me and kissed my cheek. His soft lips made my heart soar. Dizzy, I retreated from him. I scooted along the wall, back into the foyer, and climbed the staircase on tiptoes.

The witch chanted in a low voice, invoking the cut to open and the ghosts to swarm out. Then, she stopped chanting, lowered her arms, and leaned over the balcony, looking down. It was probably because of Sean, running to the circle.

"What the hell?" she muttered.

I channeled the bone's magic. "*Immobilis*," I whispered. The witch stilled. "*Converso*." Her rigid body turned around.

She regarded me with a wicked smile. "Now, now, now. What do we have here?"

I didn't waste time answering. "*Dormio*."

The witch blinked her eyes, trying to stay awake, but the bone magic won, and her eyes closed.

I let out a sigh of relief. That was easier than I thought it would be. I rushed to the edge of the balcony and looked down. Sean stood beside the circle. He looked up and gave me a thumbs up. The circle was closed and the cut was frozen. Then, his hand dropped and his eyes went wide.

"Hazel!" he yelled.

The dark witch's hands closed around my throat. "You really think a sleeping spell is going to contain me?" She cackled. "You're so naive."

She lifted me off the ground as if I weighed nothing. My throat burned and I gasped. I jerked on her grip, trying to think through the desperation rushing through me. Which spell could I use?

Before I could come up with something, she threw me off the balcony.

"*Volito*," I screamed. My fall slowed down a bit, and I hit the ground on my back. The air rushed out of my lungs.

Sean held my arms and helped me up as the dark witch floated gracefully from the balcony to the first floor.

She walked toward us. "Oh, this is going to be fun."

Sean pulled me behind him. "Stay away."

"How cute." The dark witch chuckled. "A human defending a light witch. It sounds more like a fairy tale."

She flicked her hand in Sean's direction, and he went flying to the left. He hit the wall with a huff and fell forward on his knees.

Lizzie cried, rushing at the dark witch. Not even looking at the girl, the witch raised her hand and Lizzie stopped in midair, immobile.

"I can't move," she yelled. "Let me go, you bitch!"

The dark witch laughed.

I grabbed a vial of liquid white sage from inside my

utility belt. In the process, the dagger fell to the side, but I ignored it.

"*Lux*," I said, throwing the liquid in her direction.

She raised her hand and the drops of the liquid evaporated into smoke. She cackled. "You're a novice, aren't you? Still reciting the spells and using potions to help you." She closed her eyes and took a deep breath, tilting her head back. Then her dark eyes returned to me. "Weak."

I scooted back. From the corner of my eye, I saw Sean stand and run to the dagger. He let out a cry, and then lunged at the dark witch. Once more, she waved her hand and Sean went flying away. But this time he stayed there, his back pressed to the wall and his arms outstretched beside him.

"Let him go," I said, reaching for the clasp of my belt. "I'll take off my belt. I'll be harmless, and then it's just you and me. But please, let him go."

"That is even cuter," the dark witch said. "The light witch cares about the human." She pointed her finger to Sean. Tendrils of black smoke seeped from the wall and ran over his body. A hissing sound echoed through the living room, as if the smoke was burning his clothes, his skin. He clenched his teeth, keeping the scream in.

"Please." I took off my belt and threw it in her direction. Several vials fell from the belt and spilled across the floor.

"What's the fun in that?" She closed her hand and the tendrils seeped into Sean's body.

"No!" I shouted.

"Now he has only a few minutes until the darkness reaches his heart and stops it."

"You bitch," I said through gritted teeth. I lunged at her, not really sure what I was going to do, just knowing I had to hurt her somehow.

Instead, I bumped into an invisible wall. I looked around. I was inside the white circle, *my* circle. I punched against the wall, but it was as solid as brick.

"Let's make it more fun." She snapped her fingers and wind surged from the border of the circle, closing in.

Gasping, I stepped to the center. The speed of the high wind pushed against me, and I planted my feet on the floor, trying to stay up. But the wind didn't just push against me. It also sucked all the air from the circle. I inhaled deeply, but barely any air made it into my lungs.

The dark witch looked up. "Where were we?" She raised her hands over her head, and the cut came back to life, sparking and crackling. It began opening again.

But ... the circle? The dark witch must have neutralized my circle. After all, the circle didn't close the cut; it stopped it so that I could close it.

With a loud thunder-like sound, the cut expanded, as big and wide as a basketball player. Beside it, the chandelier's light flickered—it hadn't even been on a moment ago. A swarm of ghosts slipped out from the cut, filling the room, the entire house. One of them hovered over me, laughing like a maniac. What? Seeing a witch trapped in agony was supposed to be funny? Another ghost floated toward Sean. He ran his fingers down his cheek, making Sean's body convulse.

Think, Hazel, think.

The dagger was in the circle with me, but the potions and the crystals were out of reach. Wait. I had something else. I clutched the bone pendant and focused. I wasn't afraid anymore. I couldn't be. I wouldn't be. Gasping for air, I channeled the magic within the bone.

Please, please, let it be enough.

Magic flowed into me, filling my veins, powering my core, making me strong. Holding on to this new magic, I raised my hands in front of me. "*Tardo.*" The wind slowed, then died. I took a lungful of air, steading my breathing, before I pulled my hand close then let it out, releasing a wave of power. "*Stupefacio.*"

The dark witch turned big eyes at me. "How—?"

The wave of magic hit the dark witch, throwing her to the other side of the room. I waited, ready to call out another spell, but she didn't move.

Taking advantage of the magic still in me, I looked up at the cut. "*Finis.*" The cut didn't close, but ghosts stopped coming out. I channeled more magic. "*Recedo,*" I said. The cut began sucking the ghosts back inside it. They shrieked, trying to hold on to each other, to doors, or pillars, but the magic was too strong for them.

I let the magic do its thing and turned to Sean. His sister moved to the cut, her eyes wide with terror. "*Manto,*" I said, pointing to her. She stopped moving toward the seam.

"Hazel," Sean muttered, seeing me walking to him.

"*Liber,*" I said.

His weak body fell to the ground. He turned on his back and gasped, "It hurts."

Lizzie and I knelt beside him. I put my hand on his chest. "*Curo.*" I felt the tendrils moving inside him. A little darkness emerged from his skin and clothes, but there was more. I could feel it. I focused on him again. "*Curo,*" I shouted.

Sean put his hand over mine. "It's too deep inside."

"No, no." Tears brimmed in my eyes. "*Curo!*" I yelled.

He squeezed my hand. "It's okay, Hazel." Then he smiled at Lizzie. "I know Hazel will give you peace, and soon I'll be with you."

"No." Lizzie's voice broke. "You're supposed to live. To be happy."

He gasped; his eyes rolled back in his head.

No, no.

Following the magic inside me, I put my arm around Sean's head and propped him up. I leaned into him and brushed my lips to his. A tear rolled down my cheek. I had wished to kiss him, but not like this. I pressed my lips harder to his, and he responded immediately, opening his mouth and moving it in rhythm with mine. His lips were soft and warm, and they fit mine perfectly. His tongue brushed against mine and I almost got lost in the sensation. Almost. I focused on my magic. *Egredior*, I chanted in my mind. *Egredior!* I felt the darkness moving again, coming to my command. It traveled from his torso to his throat. Noticing what I was doing, Sean tried to pull away, but I used magic to keep him still. I deepened the kiss, again fighting not to get lost in it. The darkness slid from his throat to his mouth, and then into my mouth.

The bone in my necklace shattered, and I felt the magic slipping away from me. I pulled back and picked the pieces of bone from my lap. Damn it. This was Brita's bone. How could I have broken it? The witch doctor would kill me.

Sean, now better, sat up and stared at me. "Why did you do that?" He reached for me. "Did you take it? Is it in you?" I nodded and he shook his head. "No, no."

I extended my hand between us. The darkness I had inhaled emerged from my palm. "*Abeo*," I said. The ball of darkness faded away into the air.

"You're okay?" he asked.

I smiled. "I am."

Sean cupped his hand around my neck and pulled my lips back to his. Full of energy, he kissed me, his mouth melding with mine, his tongue drawing a happy sigh from my chest. This. This was how our first kiss should have been.

Lizzie cleared her throat beside us and I pulled away. Sean kept his arm on my back.

"They are gone," Lizzie said. I looked around. "The ghosts. They are all gone."

I closed my eyes for a second and waited to feel their presence. She was right. They were all gone.

I stood. I drew the star with the hawthorn berry powder inside the circle. After finding the right vial, I poured the liquid on the floor, directly under the cut, and said, "*Finis*." The cut shrank into itself, crackling and sparking, until it was a dot. Then, it snapped and vanished. The lights on the chandelier stopped flickering and died out.

"My turn. Please, can you free me, Hazel?" Lizzie asked.

"Wait." Sean stood. "Does it have to be now? Can't you stay a little longer?"

She smiled. "I've been here for almost a year, Sean. I'm tired. And I'm guessing it's easier on Hazel to send me when it's still Friday the Thirteenth."

Technically, it was already past midnight and Friday the Thirteenth was over, but she was right. It would be easier on me if I sent her back before dawn.

I nodded.

Sean frowned. "But ... we didn't have much time together."

"We don't need it. I've been watching you for the past year when I could. I know how you were, how you felt." Lizzie touched his cheek. "Promise me you will let it go. Promise me you won't feel guilty anymore, that you will move on, and be happy."

He shook his head. "I can't ..."

"Sean, promise me. Please."

He sighed and rested his hand on hers. "I ... promise."

She kissed his cheek then turned to me. "I'm ready."

"Stand in the circle, please," I asked.

Lizzie didn't necessarily need to be in the circle, but after this night, I was tired and having her in the circle would take less magic from me. Lizzie stood in the middle of the burnt circle. I retrieved the pouch with hawthorn berry powder from the floor and held some of it in my hand. I nodded to her.

"I love you, Sean," she said.

By my side, Sean croaked, "I love you too, Lizzie."

I threw the red powder on her. "*Liberi.*"

She exploded into white smoke and evaporated in the air.

Sean stared at where she had been a second ago, a huge frown on his face.

"She's in a better place now," I told him. I didn't know how the afterlife was exactly, but I knew it was supposed to be better than being trapped in our world.

He didn't move. Not sure what else to say or do, I started gathering my vials and crystals.

Sean picked up my belt and returned it to me. "What now?"

"Now, I clean this mess."

14

BEING BACK IN THE FRENCH QUARTER MADE ME NERVOUS. After all that had happened this week, after my last time here when I had seen that supernatural store tucked in right where anyone could see it, it was hard to be here and pretend everything was normal.

However, as I walked across Bourbon Street, I didn't see any other supernaturals, didn't sense them. Probably because I had broken the bone pendant and its magic was now gone.

I took a deep breath and pushed open the door of the Midnight Cauldron. A couple of tourists walked around the front of the shop, taking pictures with odd statues and masks and such. Typical.

I weaved my way to the back, where Khalisa stood behind the counter, looking bored.

Her dark eyes shone when she saw me. "I take it you didn't die."

I smiled. "No, I didn't. And I was able to close the cut and send all the ghosts back."

She offered me her trademark crazed grin. "Well done."

I sighed, taking a small jewelry box from my jacket pocket. "There was some damage." I opened the box and showed her the necklace and the broken pieces of Brita's bone. "I'm so, so sorry. I don't know how to repay you." I was sure there was no amount of money that would fix it.

She laughed, tipping her head back. The customers eyed her suspiciously, but she ignored them. "I have a secret to tell you, child. About two hundred years ago, a witch doctor made thousands of necklaces like this one from chicken bones. She only took out one at a time, and she told her customers that it was a piece of bone from whomever she thought was popular at the time, and that it was the only one in the world. I told you it was Brita because, besides Arianna, she was one of the strongest light witches. I couldn't tell you it was Arianna since we know her bones were burned to ashes, otherwise I would have."

I gasped. "Wait. You lied to me?"

"Sure I did. And it worked."

"H-how did it work? And all that magic I channeled from it?"

"There was a bit of magic in it. Voodoo magic, but only a tiny bit so that when you touched it, you felt it was different, strong. But it wasn't. You probably used it all in one of your early spells."

"But ... I don't understand. I was able to do things I

couldn't before, things I couldn't even dream of doing."

"Because the voodoo magic I put in it is of revelation. It helped reach the magic buried in you, the magic that flows in your veins. You're powerful, Hazel, very powerful."

I touched my chest. "Magic buried in me?"

"Don't worry. It wasn't on purpose. From what I could sense, it was something in you. Maybe fear? I don't know. But you've released it now. It's unstable, but with some practice, you can reach it."

"Oh." I glanced down at me, as if I would see a different person. Nope, it was just me. But with more magic. I inhaled deeply, feeling the new magic running in me. "Wow." I had never realized I had more magic. To me, the first time my magic manifested itself was a scare, and I unconsciously shut it out. But when the second time happened, I thought that was all I had. I always believed I was weak, not that the fear of using magic was still so strong that I had kept a large amount hidden inside me. I smiled. "Thank you."

She waved me off.

I thanked her again and turned to leave.

"Where are you going now?" she asked.

I glanced over my shoulder. "To the Lightgrove coven."

I WAS EXPECTED AT THE LIGHT CASTLE. THIS TIME, TWO soldiers led me through the hallways to the council chambers, both of them dressed in all white—from the little I could gather, the difference in color meant ranking. One of them was the guy with the scar on the corner of his lips. The other was a charming guy with dark skin and long, thick hair.

Queen Denise, Clara, Grace, Amelia, and Lenora were seated on their chairs, waiting for me, along with the three familiars. Once again, they wore fine gowns as if they were going to a ball.

"Well done," Queen Denise said when I walked in.

I stopped in front of them. "What happened to the Darkmist witch?"

"We received your message and sent soldiers to take her," Lenora said. "She's being held in our dungeon. For now."

I gulped. For now. Though light witches were good, they didn't allow evil creatures to go around unpunished. They would take away her powers or execute her. I focused on something else, which wasn't necessarily better. "I probably should have told you sooner, but earlier this week, I saw two Brotherhood of Purity members at Towland." The witches exchanged glances. "I don't know what they were doing there, and once I saw them, I ran away, but ... um, I hadn't expected to find the Brotherhood in such a place. I've been a little worried about bumping into them since then."

"I understand," Queen Denise said, her voice sure. "We've heard about that and I assure you, we've taken care of that. You shouldn't worry about the Brotherhood anymore."

Easier said than done. If I passed the initiate program and joined the Lightgrove for real, I would probably worry about them a lot. But I had to trust the council, otherwise everything would be for naught.

Something else nagged at my mind. "Did you know? About the magic in me?"

The queen nodded. "We could feel it."

"Couldn't you have released it?"

"We could," she said. "But you would be stronger if you did it yourself."

I nodded, understanding. It was pretty mean to send me to a place overflowing with ghosts and a dark witch, and not being sure I would make it. But I understood that it had to be me. I had to reach for it. To feel it. To use it.

I took a deep breath, calming my nerves. "Did I pass the test?"

Queen Denise smiled. "You certainly did. Welcome to the Lightgrove coven."

My heart squeezed and I gasped. I had done it. I actually had done it.

"To the initiate program," Lenora added quickly.

It was okay. I could live with another, longer test. "Thank you," I muttered, suddenly overcome with pride of myself. Though, a new worry bloomed in me. "Um, what about my classes at Towland? Do I need to drop them?"

Once more, the council members exchanged pointed looks. I swear, they probably could read each other's minds.

Finally, the queen said, "We'll allow you to continue your classes at Towland."

I beamed. That was more than I was expecting, and I would take it all gladly.

"A few other girls have become of age too," Lenora continued, clearly oblivious that I was in heaven. "We'll hold a welcoming ceremony for all of you in two weeks."

The double doors opened and a young woman stepped inside. She also wore an elegant gown and she had a big smile on her face.

"This is my daughter, Marjorie," Queen Denise said. "She'll give you a quick tour of the castle and show you to your future bedroom."

My jaw slacked. "My room?"

"Yes. After the ceremony, the Light Castle will be your new home," Queen Denise said. "You don't need to sleep here every night, since it might not be convenient with your early classes, but you're welcome to come and go anytime."

My heart swelled. They would allow me to finish my degree even though I wouldn't need one if I was working for them. I had never allowed myself to dream about joining them before, but I was sure that if I had, it wouldn't have been this good.

"Thank you," I whispered, afraid that if I spoke up, I would cry.

They nodded and I took that as my cue to leave. I walked to the door.

"Hi, there, I'm Marjorie," the girl said. She probably wasn't much older than I was.

"Hi, I'm Hazel."

She offered me a sweet smile. "Follow me. I'll show you around."

I exited the room with Marjorie and the doors once

again closed by themselves. "They always do that?"

Marjorie chuckled. "Yes. They have magic imbued in them to open and close when needed."

I glanced at the doors again. That was amazing.

I wondered if the castle was under attack, would the doors shut and stay like that no matter what? I shivered. Hopefully, no one knew and would never have to find out.

Just then, loud footsteps echoed down the long hallway. Two women in black leather clothes walked down the hallway with sure steps, even though they were surrounded by six of the Light Order soldiers.

Doreen and Norah.

Right, they had told me they had an audience with the Lightgrove council on Saturday. I hadn't realized I would be seeing them again.

Marjorie and I stepped to the side and let them pass. Behind us, the double doors opened again. When they were right by my side, Doreen and Norah glanced at me. Norah smiled and Doreen winked.

Then, they disappeared into the council room, and the doors closed once more.

"Do you know them?" Marjorie asked, her smile smaller. She was intrigued.

Truth was, so was I.

I frowned. "No, I don't." It wasn't a lie. I might have met them but I didn't really know them. I was glad they hadn't lied to me, though. I sighed and squared my shoulders. "So, you were going to show me my room?"

"Right." Marjorie regained her composure and smiled wide again. "Right this way."

15

I brushed my hair in front of the mirror.

Krissa stood behind me and wolf-whistled. "You look great for someone just going to class on a Monday morning."

I shrugged, checking my outfit once more. It wasn't too different from my normal clothes, but I made a point of dressing up a bit. A dark red blouse, fake leather leggings, and high-heel boots. I applied the same amount of makeup I always wore, but this time tried a pale pink gloss on my lips, and made sure I had sprayed my favorite perfume on my neck.

Maybe it was futile, but after Friday the Thirteenth, I wasn't sure what was going on between Sean and me, and if dressing up a little helped me find out, so be it.

After we left the haunted mansion, we had walked back to campus side by side. We didn't say much, but I could feel the change in him, as if the weight was gone from his shoulders. When we arrived at my building, he bid me goodnight and left. Nothing else. I confess my heart sank a little. I was kind of hoping for a goodnight kiss.

Regardless, today was a new day and the possibilities were endless.

"You're smiling," Krissa said. "A sweet smile. That's new too."

I chuckled. "Yeah, yeah." What did she know about me? We had been roommates for only ten-ish days.

I picked up my purse, waved goodbye, and left the room.

Giddy, I raced down the stairs and rushed out the front door. I stopped dead in my tracks, my heart skipping a beat. Sean stood on the sidewalk, smoking a cigarette, and he looked ... wow. He had on dark jeans and a black hoodie that hugged his strong shoulders. His hair, though, was as messy as always, and I liked it.

He saw me, took a last drag of his cigarette before throwing it away, and a lopsided smile appeared on his lips. His face was still marred by the bruises from his showdown at the bar, but it didn't lessen the impact of his beauty. He ran a hand through his hair then grabbed two coffee to-go cups from the top of a short brick wall behind him, and walked up to me.

"Hi," I said, a little nervous.

"Hey." He handed me one of the to-go cups. "White mocha latte."

My favorite. I gaped. "How did you know?"

He shrugged and motioned toward campus.

After taking a sip of my precious coffee, I skipped

down the dorm's front steps and walked with him side by side.

"So," Sean started after a minute or so in silence.

I looked up at him. "So?"

"Did you pass the test?"

I smiled. "Yes. The welcoming ceremony will be in two weeks." I told him about the castle and having my own bedroom there.

A crease appeared on his forehead. "You will move out of the dorm, then?"

"Oh, no. They will let me stay in the dorms. I'll just need to sleep there a couple of times during the week."

After a few more steps, Sean sighed. "What do you think happened to Doug?"

"I don't know. If you want, I can search the city for him. I mean, I'll be around anyway. I can keep my eye out for him."

"You would do that?"

I shrugged. "Why not?"

"I want to go with you."

"But—"

"No buts. I don't care if you have magic and I don't. I'll find a way of defending myself." His eyes had such a determined glint, it was hard to argue with him. Yes, I feared for him, being among supernatural beings without any magic to protect himself, but I was glad about the prospect of having company while out looking for ghosts. Especially if the company was a tall boy with wide shoulders, strong arms, bright blue eyes, and a smile that could melt my worries away.

I opened my mouth to tell him I would think about it when a black cat jumped from a nearby tree, landing right in front of me. My heart in my throat, I yelled and stumbled back. Sean, who also had been given quite a scare by the out-of-nowhere cat, stepped back and took a hold of my arm before I could make a bigger fool of myself and land on my butt.

"Jeez," I muttered. "Stupid cat." The cat meowed, but stayed there, looking at me as if it was studying me. "Shoo, kitty," I said, but the cat didn't move.

Sean tugged my arm and we walked around the cat.

"What the hell was that about?" I glanced back and the cat was still there. A few other students walked from the dorm toward campus and had to walk around him too. Totally clueless cat.

Sean let go of my arm. "A late Friday the Thirteenth prank," he teased.

"Shut up." I slapped his chest.

He put his hand over his chest and let out a fake "Ouch!"

I laughed and he smiled. And just like that, I lost my smile and focused on the path ahead of us, totally self-conscious.

"So," Sean started again.

"So," I said, growing curious about what he wasn't saying.

He finally turned to me, looking deeply into my eyes. "I was wondering if you would like to go out with me sometime." He ran a hand through his messy hair. "You know, on a date."

I bit back a smile. So, there was where we stood. I was okay with that. "I would love that."

A hint of a smile spread across his lips. "Good."

Just then a strange power surged around us, and I halted, stiffening.

"What is it?" Sean asked.

I closed my eyes and let my witch sense do its work. The power came from my right, and by its feel, it was definitely a ghost. I glanced to my right and saw a narrow alley between two old dorm buildings.

I stepped toward the alley. "I ... just ..."

"A ghost?"

"Yes."

"Let's go. Do your thing before the ghost disappears."

Smiling, I turned around and stepped into the alley with Sean following close behind. I was so lucky. I had discovered my magic, I had joined the Lightgrove coven, and I had found a guy who knew what I was, what I could do, and he was okay with it. Finally, I could think of having a real relationship, where I didn't need to hide who I was.

The power spiked and I focused on my task. I picked the pouch with the hawthorn berry powder from my pocket and prepared to free this ghost.

flew past me, leaving me a little disoriented.

Between classes, getting ready for the initiate program, and a surprise visit from Amanda and my mom, Sean and I had barely seen each other. But we walked to and from our class together, we had lunch together twice, and we texted throughout the day.

In one of our many conversations, Sean told me he was a second degree black belt in Taekwondo—hence the belts I had seen at his apartment—and he had abandoned the sport after Lizzie's and Doug's deaths. But now he was ready to move on, so he visited his old dojang and signed up for classes. I could see in the way his shoulders were relaxed and the easy smile on his lips that he was on the right path.

Moments like this one showed me his bad boy facade was only that. A facade.

Though I was happy for him, I was also a little frustrated. Now he had martial arts classes three evenings per week. And he had mentioned participating in tournaments again, which usually took all weekend.

Who was I to complain about that? Wouldn't I start having classes and training at the Light Castle too?

Just the thought made me nervous.

After my last class on Friday, I stopped by the coffee shop to buy a white mocha latte before taking the bus to Oak Hill to spend the weekend with my mother and sister —it was my mother's birthday.

As I expected, Jane was there, but she didn't look her chipper self when she took my order.

"I heard the news," she said, her tone bitter. She scribbled my name on the to-go cup and started my drink. "You made the Lightgrove coven initiate program. Congratulations."

I glanced side-to-side, making sure no one was too close to hear us. "Thanks," I said. A sliver of guilt made its way into me. I had never wanted this life and now here I was, taking it, while Jane had dreamed about this over and over again. I felt so bad for her. "I'm sorry," I whispered.

She stayed quiet while she worked on my drink. It was only when she handed me my cup that she finally met my eyes again and said, "I don't need your pity."

I took my drink and opened my mouth to say something, to mend things. I had no idea what I would have said. I just knew I didn't want her to be mad at me, but she called out the next in line and turned her attention from me.

Holding on to my drink, I forced myself out of the

coffee shop and also forced out the guilt feeling to stay there too. This wasn't my fault. I hadn't done it on purpose. I wasn't that evil.

With that in mind, I braced myself and left New Orleans behind.

***

Since the moment I got home Friday night, my mother had glued herself to me and pampered me every second of the night and day. If it weren't her birthday weekend, I would have told her to leave me alone. If it weren't her birthday weekend, I wouldn't even have come to Oak Hill.

My childhood hadn't been bad, but it hadn't been the best either. Growing up in a small town with an even smaller community of witches who liked to show off at every corner had been hell. And what blew my mind was the fact that none of them was too powerful, and yet they fought for every ounce of power and prowess, eager to show off.

On Saturday afternoon, my mother had a few friends over for tea, and of course, the main topic of their conversation was that I had made it into the Lightgrove initiate program, something no one had even dreamed of achieving.

She paraded me as if I was the newest piece of decoration in the house.

When the last group was finally leaving, I walked into the kitchen and started helping Amanda clean up. She had been oddly quiet since I had arrived the previous night, and I wondered what was bugging her.

"Hey," I muttered, approaching her. I took some dirty plates to the sink, where she was washing the dishes and loading the dishwasher. "Are you okay?"

She shrugged. "I guess. Why?"

She didn't meet my eyes. My sister was two years older than me, and though we had completely different personalities, we had been close. For a long time, she had been my best friend and I had been hers.

I remembered when we were younger, people thought we were twins. She had the same body build as mine—slim and short—and the same wispy blond hair, though she'd worn hers cut into a long bob for a few years now. Her eyes were a darker green shade than mine, and she had no piercings and tattoos. She also wore a lot of pink and baby blues. To me, she was the perfect daughter, the perfect sister, but for some reason, she never saw it that way. She was always striving to be better.

I sighed. "Talk to me, Amanda. I can see something is bothering you." I went to the other side of her, grabbed a dishtowel, and start drying the pile of dishes that remained on the drying rack. Amanda would need the space with the number of dirty dishes piling the counter. When she didn't say anything, I blurted out, "Are you mad at me too? Are you jealous?"

She finally lifted her gaze to me. "Who else is jealous?"

"Ah-ha, so you admit it. You are jealous."

She groaned, looking at the sink again. "I *am* jealous. Wouldn't you be? But I'm also happy for you." Her hands stilled. "I know you didn't plan for this, but I know you'll rock it."

"You're being sincere, right? You're not just saying that because you feel like you have to, right?"

One corner of her lips curved up and she threw a few drops of water at me. "I'm being sincere, bitch." I gasped, both from the water spilling on me and the name calling. "Now work. We still have another dinner to prepare."

With a smile, I shut up and went back to work. We cleaned up the kitchen and started dinner—a salmon casserole our grandmother used to bake for our birthdays. Now we were making it for our mother.

After a quiet but quaint dinner just the three of us, my mom, Amanda, and I moved on to the living room, where we opened a wine bottle and drank while munching on chocolate caramel kernels Amanda had made this morning. Finally, we shared our present with our mother.

It was a large painting of the three of us, inspired by a picture we had taken before I had left for New Orleans in June. Amanda knew of this artist who was wonderful with pictures, and I had to admit, the painting was better than the original.

My mother held on to the painting and her eyes filled with tears. "This is wonderful," she said, her voice breaking. She placed the painting over the coffee table and turned to me. "But the biggest gift I could ever want was you joining the Lightgrove coven."

I squirmed under her gaze. Beside me, Amanda let out a long sigh.

"Mom, I haven't officially joined them," I reminded her. "I was accepted into the initiate program."

My mom waved me off. "Potato, potahto. I'm sure you'll do great. You'll wow them and will soon be among their official ranks."

I frowned. It wouldn't be that easy and she knew it. The program was intense and designed to eliminate the candidates as time went by. At least, that was what I had heard. I didn't know much about the program, just rumors.

I drained my wineglass as my mother went on about what an honor it was to have me there, and about the ceremony next weekend, when I would be welcomed into the castle, etc.

Meanwhile, my mind wandered. From a young age, I knew I wasn't witch material. I had already accepted I would live as a human, albeit with a side ghost-hunting business. That was why I had insisted on going to New Orleans and study at a human college, where I could be human.

Then, this opportunity with the Lightgrove witches showed up and I couldn't deny I was excited about it. But I tried to understand my excitement. Was it because I had done something no one expected of me? Something I hadn't expected of myself? Was it because this new phase was unknown and charming and mysterious? Or was it because my mother's excitement molded mine? What if I couldn't care less about being a Lightgrove witch and I was doing this to make my mother proud?

I couldn't tell the difference anymore.

Lost and confused, I poured more wine into my glass.

"Although, Hazel," my mother went on, "you have to do something about this." She gestured to me.

I glanced down at myself. "What do you mean?"

"No respectable witch has streaked hair, or that many piercings and tattoos," she said, suddenly condescending. "And what's going on with your clothes? So much black."

I brought my glass to my lips and drank it all in one go, drowning the retort threatening to spill over. If I said something now, I knew I would later regret it. So I drank my wine and when that was gone, I pretended to get an important call and excuse myself.

My feelings swirled inside me as I dragged my feet to my bedroom. For a moment there, when my mother was criticizing me, I almost gave up. I almost told her I was doing all of this for her, and if she couldn't support me, who I was, then I wouldn't do it.

But my gut had tightened at the thought, which told me I was divided about joining the Lightgrove coven. Was I doing this for my mother or for myself? I didn't know anymore.

When I was alone in the dark of my bedroom, I lay in bed and texted Sean.

I miss you.

I waited, staring at the screen for an answer.

But none came.

Holding on to my phone and waiting, I fell asleep.

17

The bedroom was large with a high rounded ceiling. The four-posted silk-sheeted bed on the right could fit five or six of me. On the left, a matching blue velvet couch and armchair took most of the space, save for the large wooden desk and chair. And let's not forget the balcony over-looking the downhill side of a nameless mountain and the closet. A room bigger than my college dorm, with floor-to-ceiling wooden shelves covering every inch of the walls, filled with party gowns. And it was all mine. The bedroom, the balcony, the view, and the gowns. All mine.

But there was a special one, dressed on a real-size mannequin in the middle of my closet—the one I was supposed to put on for the event this evening. The event that would begin in less than an hour.

And even though I had my hair (a side braid) and my makeup done, I still couldn't make myself pick up that beautiful, beautiful dress from the mannequin.

I stood there, frozen under the doorjamb, staring at the dress that should be worn by a princess, not me. Not tattooed, pierced, streaked hair me.

Since my mother's birthday last weekend, I had felt queasy and insecure about this new path in my life. I had asked myself over and over again, why I was doing this? Was it because of my mother, or because I really wanted it?

I still couldn't answer that question.

My cell phone vibrated against my hip and I jumped, my heart accelerating for ten seconds. Slowly, I picked the phone from the front pocket of my jeans and read the text.

I wish I was there with you.

My insides warmed up and I felt like hugging my phone. Since he saw me using my magic to send ghosts back to their world and defeat a dark witch on Friday the Thirteenth two weeks ago, Sean had become a lifeline I didn't know I needed. Unfortunately, this past week hadn't been any different from the previous one. Our college classes and Sean's martial arts classes made us both busy at different hours, and we had barely spent any time together. Sometimes I wondered if this too was doomed to fail, but I wasn't ready to give this up yet. I wanted this, whatever this was, to work.

Me too.

Good luck. Call me tomorrow.

Thanks. I will.

I stared at the phone for a couple of minutes, expecting another reply, but when none came. I stashed my phone back into my pocket and forced myself to face the gown in front of me once more.

This was childish. Why was I so afraid of a damn dress? What could it do? Curse me? Besides, it would be fun to dress up for a night, to dance in a castle's ballroom and pretend I was really living a fairy tale. Wouldn't it?

I sighed, wishing once more that Sean was here with me. To parade and dance with me. Then, it would certainly be a fairy tale.

A knock on the door startled me and I turned to it.

"Hazel? Are you there?"

It was my sister, Amanda.

Like a soldier on a mission, I walked to my bedroom's door and opened it.

"Hey," I said, stepping aside so she could get in. Her eyes shone with pure mischief as she walked in my bedroom, carrying a giant white box. Her long bob was neatly combed over her shoulders. "What are you up to?"

She smiled. "Why do you think I'm up to something?"

I pointed to her face. "Because I know that face."

A small knot appeared on her forehead. "What face?"

I kept on my finger pointed, gesturing to every inch of her face. "That expression. It's your I've-got-a-crazy-idea expression." At least Amanda seemed more relaxed since our short talk last weekend. Perhaps she had accepted this was happening, and instead of feeling jealous, she would support me and be the best sister anyone could have.

At least, that was what I hoped was happening here.

She pretended to gasp. "I do not have an I've-got-a-crazy-idea face."

I crossed my arms. "You do!"

She harrumphed and dropped the box over my bed. "Fine. But look at this then you yell at me if you want."

If I knew my sister well, this—whatever it was—would get me in trouble, but I couldn't shake off my curiosity.

"What is it?" I asked, reaching for the box.

My sister rolled up, shifting her weight from her toes to the balls of her feet, as if she was about to jump in excitement, but was trying to hold back. "Look inside," she said.

Biting my lower lip, I pulled the box lid off one tiny inch and peeked inside. Shiny, black fabric stared back at me. I then pushed the lid off completely and picked up the fabric, holding it at an arm's length from me.

I sucked in a shallow breath. "Holy shit," I muttered as my eyes rummage every inch of the fanciest, most beautiful party gown I had ever seen. "What is this?"

"Well," Amanda started, walking to my closet's door. "Even though I would love to wear a dress like that"—she pointed to the princess like dress on the mannequin—"I know you wouldn't. So, I brought you a dress I knew you would like."

I folded the dress in my arms and stared at her. "But ... why ... how did you know? How did you know I wouldn't like that dress?" I jerked my chin toward the close.

She lifted one shoulder, dismissively. "I'm your sister,

and despite all our fights and arguments, I know you better than anyone else. I knew you wouldn't feel comfortable in whatever the White Sisterhood told you to wear."

Something like awe filled my chest. I had never expected this from my sister. "Thank you."

She waved a hand at me. "No need to thank me. Just put the damn thing on so we can get going."

In a haste, I walked into the closet and put on the dress. Amanda helped pull and push all the pieces into place, then I turned to the full-length mirror and gasped. The dress was in some ways simple but inventive and utterly gorgeous. It was basically a strapless black tube going from the top of my breasts to the middle of my thighs, and then the magic happened: a gossamer-like fabric in glittery black came from one of my shoulders, twisted around my waist and opened to a flowy skirt that brushed the floor. A side slit appear, showing my leg from foot to thigh, each time I moved. It was the most beautiful dress I had ever seen. I put on my lace black boots to finish the ensemble.

"Whoa," Amanda said from behind me. She was watching me through the mirror.

"I have to admit, I even look pretty in this dress."

She laughed. "You're always pretty, Hazel. The dress just emphasizes that."

I waved her off. She was always nice to me and handed me compliments right and left, even when I didn't deserve them.

Without giving much thought to it, I picked up my cell phone, snapped a pic of me in front of the mirror, and sent it to Sean.

I bit my lips, waiting for his reply.

"What are you doing?" Amanda asked, trying to glance at my phone.

I hid the phone behind me. "Nothing."

She tilted her head to the side and put her hands on her waist. "Hazel Rose Levine! Hiding your phone behind your back? Now I know it's not nothing."

We would probably have kept acting like children— her chasing me, and me hiding the phone—but the phone vibrated in my hand, and holding my breath, I stared at the screen.

> Wow … Sorry it took me so long to answer, but I was staring at the picture.

> So … you like it?

> I do. Very much. You look stunningly hot.

I blushed and wondered how to answer his text.

"Tell him he's hot," my sister said. She was glued to my side, watching the screen with me. "Wait, is he hot?" The warmth on my cheeks increased and her smile widened. "Oh, I see he is hot. I demand to see pictures."

I was about to type a quick, lame "Thanks" when a new text came in.

> I just realized the ceremony tonight is a ball, right? And there will probably be lots of guys there, right? Man … Now I REALLY wish I was there.

"Aw, he's so cute," Amanda cooed.

I was sure my cheeks were bright red.

I really wish you were here too.

A knock came from the door, followed by a deep voice. "The ceremony starts in ten minutes."

On cue, my hands started sweating and trembling, and my breathing became shallow. I wasn't one to be nervous too often, but tonight was a big night and I didn't remember being this nervous ever before.

Amanda took my cell phone from me and gave me one last examining look. "You look gorgeous and you'll do great." She embraced me. "Congratulations, little sister. I'm happy for you."

My chest filled with awe and appreciation one more time. At this rate, I would be in tears even before the ceremony started.

I pulled back and smiled at her. "Thanks."

She interlaced her fingers with mine and tugged my arm. "Now come on. Let's enjoy your big night."

18

In the hallway, a member of the Light Order told Amanda to go to the ballroom and wait for the ceremony, then he ushered me to what looked like a sitting room outside the ballroom, with velvet loveseats and low tables with fancy finger food.

All the new girls were gathered there—fifteen total— and I felt all of their eyes on me as I entered the room. I wondered if it was because of my tattoos and piercings and streaked hair, or because of my dress. After all, they were all wearing the princess gown the Lightgrove had given them. The gowns were exactly like the one standing alone at my closet right now, except for the color. All gown shades were slightly different, varying from off-white to dark blue. But none were black.

Or they could be staring because of everything about me.

An uneasy feeling settled in my belly. If I lowered my resolve, this moment could have suffocated me. I had been so unsure about joining the Lightgrove coven, about going through the initiate program, about doing my best here and trying to become a real witch. Now, with these intense, curious, and reproaching stares, I wondered if I should be here.

Maybe I didn't belong here at all.

"Hi," I said meekly. A few girls said hello back, others waved, and others turned their heads as if I was nothing more than a nasty fly on the wall.

Before I could find a seat or stand beside some random girl and start small talk—because really, I had to try—two Light Order soldiers entered the room. They stood by the large doors, rigid like statues, and then Queen Denise walked in, looking powerful and imposing in her fancy, full skirt and puffy sleeved white gown. She looked more like a fairy queen than the queen of a witch coven and the leader of the council.

The queen smiled at us. If she was bothered by my appearance, she didn't show it. "Good evening, ladies. Are you ready?" There were half-mumbled "yes" coming from every direction. "That didn't sound convincing. Anyway, we're ready to receive you." She walked across the room, her guards on her tail, where a set of heavy, wooden double doors stood. She paused in front of the doors. "Please, enter the ballroom as I call your name. Go down the stairs and stop in front of the council forming a single line."

The guards pushed both doors open and Queen Denise walked out, disappearing from sight after a left turn. From here, all I could see was the rounded ceiling and several heavy, metal chandeliers holding hundreds of flickering candles.

Then, the queen's voice boomed through the air, calling the first name.

A girl with blonde curls who didn't look older than sixteen squealed and rushed to the open double doors. She stopped before crossing them, straightened her back, and plastered a big smile on her face. Then she walked out and turned left.

Queen Denise called the second name, and the third, and the fourth ...

"Hazel Rose Levine," her voice echoed through the room and I stifled a gasp. I didn't know why it surprised me to hear my name, since I was expecting it, but it did. Not only did it surprised me, but it also made me incredibly nervous.

I took a deep breath and walked out of the room.

The next hour went by in a blur. I remember going down the stairs, under bright lights and curious stares. I remember lining up with the other girls, being greeted and welcomed by the council, taking turns while the other girls and I received a white brooch (it was only a pentagram, without the rune in the center like the full members had) that marked us as Lightgrove initiates, a big toast, and cheer after the important part was done, and the music playing through the ballroom, indicating that the party had started.

My mother and Amanda came rushing to me and embraced me—Amanda was smiling wide and my mother was crying happy tears.

"Amanda, I think you overdid it," I whispered in her ear. "Everyone is staring at me. I'm not dressed like anyone else in here."

She clicked her tongue. "Of course they are staring. You look stunning, and like yourself, not like some spoiled princess. Be proud, little sister. You're one of a kind." She winked and raised her champagne glass to me.

I smiled and took a glass of champagne for myself.

A young waitress walked around with trays full of drinks and food. Even at the many tables, the food never seemed to disappear, even though I could see everyone eating the little bites. The only thing I could think was that it was magic keeping the plates and trays replenished.

Soon, the dance floor was filling up fast with the witches and the soldiers of the Light Order. Even the new members of the coven were being asked to dance.

Beside me, Amanda cleared her throat. I was about to ask what her deal was when a guy halted in front of me. The Light Order soldier with the tiny scar on the corner of his lips.

He bowed his head and offered his hand to me. "May I have this dance?"

I opened my mouth to say no, when Amanda nudged me on the back, pushing me to him. "Of course you may," she said for me as the guy caught my elbows and held me up before I kissed the floor. Or his chest.

Without waiting for my word, he caught my hand and pulled me to the dance floor. I shot a glare to Amanda— she knew about Sean!—but she laughed and waved me off.

The guy steered me to him, and I gently placed one of

my hands on his shoulder, while he caught the other in his large, warm palm. Then he placed his other hand on my waist and I stiffened.

"No need to be nervous," he said, his eyes staring holes into mine. "You are stunning and everyone should be staring you." My cheeks warmed up and he smiled. I had seen him before, but only now I paid attention to him. Tall, with short blond hair, and goldish-hazel eyes. This guy was handsome in his own right. "I'm Rodd, captain of the Third Battalion of the Light Order."

"I'm—"

"Hazel Rose Levine. I bet everyone here knows your name."

The heat in my cheeks only increased. "I prefer not drawing that much attention to myself."

"Too late."

Self-conscious from his intense stare, I scanned the room as we spun around it. Girls danced and chatted and laughed with guys from the Light Order, a few older couples danced, while others stayed at the edge of the dance floors, talking and observing. The council members occupied a table along one of the walls of the ballroom. Several people milled about them, and several Light Order members stood guard around them.

Even though there were family members present for the ceremony, like my mother and my sister, there were only a handful of males that weren't part of the Light Order. I wondered what the rules here were, and if I could have brought Sean with me after all.

What was I thinking? Sean and I were not a couple ...

yet? I wasn't sure what we were, but we certainly weren't girlfriend and boyfriend, though I hoped we would get to that point soon, and then, I would make sure I learned the rules about bringing males to the castle, because I wanted Sean to be here with me for the next important event.

"I hear you aren't a legacy," Rodd said, pulling me back into the now. "But I heard you surprised the council with your deeds."

I scoffed. Surprised the council with my deeds? That was new. "Where did you hear that?"

He lifted one shoulder. "Word gets around the castle fast."

Great. So there were rumors and gossiping around the castle. Good to know.

I raised my chin, not afraid of the rumors. To me, not being a legacy was a small issue I didn't intend to care about. "Don't believe everything you hear."

One corner of his lips curled up. "I'll keep that in mind."

The song ended, and before the next one could start, I took a step back, forcing Rodd to let go of me. "Thanks for the dance," I said, grasping for a reasonable excuse. "But I—"

Thunder echoed through the air and everyone gasped.

In the middle of the dance floor, black light cut from the ceiling to the floor, rapid sizzles like lightning, one after another, loud and bright and powerful. The people who had been dancing three seconds ago, scurried back, leaving a wide berth to the crackling light.

Rodd had his hand on my arm and pulled me behind him, protecting me from whatever that was.

The council members assembled a circle around the black light, and behind them the Light Order.

"I have to go with them," Rodd said, glancing at me over his shoulder. "Please, stay back."

He let go of me and rushed to the line with the other men who composed the top ranking soldiers. Then Amanda and my mother had their hands on me and pulled me back.

"What's happening?" Amanda asked. "Is this part of the ceremony?"

"I have no idea," I whispered, gawking as the black light changed. It became more fluid, smoother, but equally hot and loud and alarming. They looked like flames but pitch black. Smoke rose from the scorched floor.

I expected the council witches to do something. To cast a spell and stop the fire, or anything else that would make sense of whatever was happening, but they just stood there, staring at the fire—poised to attack, but not really moving.

After a few minutes, the sound was quieter, the length of the flames not as high, the heat not as strong, and then they were gone.

The entire ballroom was quiet.

Everyone stared at the marred floor, at the not so random dark marking the black fire had left behind.

"What's that?" Amanda whispered in my ear.

A broken arrow with half of its feathers, and a third of a circle around it.

"It's ... Arianna's rune."

She frowned. "And what does that mean?"

"I'm not sure ..." I looked around the room, at the severity of the queen's and the council's faces. Dread grew inside of me. "But it can't be good."

Continue reading Hazel's adventures with book 2, *The Midnight Spell*!

BONUS: want to read an exclusive scene from Sean's POV? Download it here!

To read a special and exclusive book about another light witch, join my Facebook Group and find the book called *The Light Witch* to download on the "featured" tab!

Flip the page to read a short story about Arianna's death—the founder of the Lightgrove Witches!

THE MIDNIGHT FIRE

(previously titled *Into the Darkest Fire*)

An unfamiliar force brushed against her, licking down her spine, chilling her warm body.

They are close.

Getting tired to the point of not caring, Arianna stopped running and put her hand on a tree trunk, trying to catch her breath without collapsing.

Beside her, the soldier, Hugo, huffed. He grabbed her arm and jerked her away from the tree.

"No time to rest, m'lady," he said, his tone harsh. "They are gaining on us and I'm afraid that without a horse and —" He looked up to the darkening sky above the thick leaves. "—in the dark, we won't have much chance."

Arianna opened her mouth to argue, but the necklace resting on the cleavage of her fine dress tingled with heat.

She looked down in time to see the shine flash twice then disappear. A warning. But a warning against what?

The soldier's eyes went wide and he released her arm as if she was a monster.

No, not a monster.

A witch.

As she truly was.

For a second, she wondered if he would ignore his master's order and run away from her, leaving her alone to fend for herself. But she knew he wouldn't. Thales had assured her Hugo was the best, and one of his most trusted soldiers.

The crumbled note in her hand felt rough against her skin, and she wanted to corrode it with her mind. She glanced at it, willing the words to be different. Even if she changed them with her magic, it wouldn't matter. They wouldn't be true.

She raised her eyes to Hugo's face and found him eyeing the note. Her grip tightened around it.

With another huff, Hugo jerked his chin toward the dark beyond the trees.

After stashing the note in the pocket of the girdle around her waist, Arianna raised her skirt from the dirty ground. "Let's go."

One hour passed and they still ran.

With a small torch in one hand, Hugo kept his sword drawn in the other and slashed at the leaves and twigs, clearing a path through the woods for them to pass through safety. According to him, the horses of their pursuers wouldn't be able to pass through here. If they wanted to catch her so badly, they would have to come on foot, and that would give them a little more time.

Still, that knowledge didn't help with her fatigue.

Arianna tripped over a raised root and fell to her hands and knees. Her wish was to just stay there, to sprawl herself on the ground and sleep, even if only for a few minutes. Her legs hurt and breathing burned her lungs. She couldn't take much more of this.

Hugo put a hand on her elbow and hoisted her to her feet as if she were a weightless child.

Arianna smoothed out the skirt of her dress, hoping she hadn't ruined it. It had been a gift from Thales, and she had chosen to wear it this morning because she would spend the day at the palace, in conference with the king. After all, she was a powerful piece of his game.

However, before she could leave the town and reach the palace gates, everything went wrong.

Arianna looked down at her skirt. Oh, moon. How could she care about her dress when she was trying to escape?

"Do you have any idea where you're taking me?"

"To safety," the soldier said, resuming his march.

Even with his torch, the woods seemed too dark, too evil. Arianna could feel it, the powers and the souls roaming around the trees, just observing what they were doing and where they were going. Although, whenever she glanced to the sides, she only met darkness.

She shuddered then repressed the fear building in her chest. "And where is safety exactly?" Hugo didn't answer as he cut down an entire small tree and stepped over it. He turned to her and offered his hand. Arianna crossed her arms and raised her chin. "Where's safety?"

His shoulder's sagged and he huffed. "I don't know, m'lady."

At least he is honest. Arianna took his hand and crossed over the fallen tree, trying to think of the power it had possessed. Now it was dead because of her.

Where was safety? Would they just walk deeper into the woods until their chasers gave up? Across the woods? The villages and towns beyond the woods? Would they stop before they crossed the country's border?

Arianna shook her head. She had to focus on the present, on each of the steps she took, on each minute that passed. She was still free and safe and alive.

She just hoped her family was safe and alive too. In the note Thales sent her, he promised he would take care of her mother and her sister. Besides, he'd assured her that nobody knew who they were, and she believed him.

And there was the Lightgrove coven. The Lightgrove witches protected their members, and the ones they loved. As its founder, she had been adamant about the rule. She *knew* the Sisters were safe and would take her family with them, if Thales failed.

The unfamiliar sensation returned and brushed against her once more, stronger this time, the chill reaching her bones and freezing her in place.

Slowly, she glanced around, trying to make out any movement or figures within the dark.

A few seconds later, Hugo noticed she wasn't following him and returned to her. "M'lady, what is it?"

She put her fingers to her lips and closed her eyes. Holding her necklace, she tried to steady her heart and breathing to better control her magic and push it toward their surroundings, to search and find whatever had her on edge.

Something fell on her chest. She yelled and jumped, her heart pounding against her ribs, as Hugo helped the cat off her.

"If we weren't in such a dire situation," he said, a small smile tugging at the corners of his lips, "that would have been entertaining."

Her black cat, Shade, purred and rubbed his side against the skirt of her dress.

"Stupid cat," she hissed. With a hand over her heart, Arianna leaned against a tree and tried to calm her nerves. "I thought I felt something." Shaking her head, she smiled. "Leave it to a cat to put the witch to shame."

Hugo's wince at the word *witch* didn't escape her. The grip around the hilt of his sword tightened. "We're almost to the other side of the woods." He glanced up and she followed his gaze. A bright, beautiful full moon shone from between the leaves. "We should keep going so we can cross the bridge to the next village while it is still dark."

"You expect me to keep walking for what?" She counted in her head, trying to estimate the hour using the moon's position. "Four more hours?"

He raised his torch high, but it didn't illuminate more than a couple of feet around them, and started walking again. "I would say five."

This time, Arianna was the one who huffed before stalking behind him.

The sensation that something was around them hadn't fade. It hadn't been Shade. It was something else. She could feel its thick evil claws floating along the edge of the darkness, following them, observing where she was being taken, and waiting for the right moment to attack.

Shuddering, she turned her eyes from the darkness and rushed closer to the soldier.

***

ARIANNA STUMBLED FORWARD AND ALMOST FELL, BUT regained her footing and sighed. Her eyelids were heavy and she struggled to stay awake.

But each time her eyes closed, the images that burned behind them shook her awake.

She could still see the moment as if she were still there, the hooded men arriving on their horses, soldiers behind them, the villagers hiding their wives and daughters. The hooded men brought everyone together in the central square, as if they were cattle, and asked them, "Who is the Light Witch?" One of them spat on the feet of a young woman with pale skin, long auburn hair, and green eyes. Just like her.

But Thales had seen them coming and had ordered Hugo to take her away. She saw it all from under a wagon, being carried out of town, as the women were tied to posts and interrogated.

Then, when Hugo had taken her up the hill, she saw the fire starting and heard the screams and cries. She ran back to the hill, screaming, "I'm here. Let them alone!" But Hugo's arms closed around her waist and hoisted her away.

She put her hands on her ears and crouched, fighting the sobs that shook her chest.

"What are you doing?" Hugo's voice crashed into her nightmare.

Arianna snapped her eyes open and looked around as Shade licked her hand.

The village was behind them. The women and young girls killed. Their cries and screams ceased, but forever imprinted on her mind.

The darkness of the woods closed in on her. She knew then what lurked in the dark, following her. The ghosts of those women and girls. She shivered as the wind bellowed around her, bringing in their whispers and curses. They would haunt her until the day she died.

Did Thales think she would want to stay alive after so many died in her place?

Oblivious to it all, Hugo extended a hand to her. "We're close."

Wiping a tear away, Arianna took his hand and stood. As soon as she was able to stop running, she would perform a passing ritual for those women, even if she didn't know all their names.

How long would this damned witch hunting season

last? How many lives would it take? And she *knew* most women and girls taken weren't witches. Not that witches deserved to die, either.

Arianna fell into step behind Hugo and noticed he didn't rush as much as before.

After a few more minutes, he stopped and raised his hand. Arianna froze, afraid of what he had seen, or not seen.

He turned to her, sweeping the torch close to her face, and she jumped back, eyes wide. Didn't he know that fire could burn her magic away?

"We're here," he whispered.

"Here where?" she asked in an equally hushed voice.

Without answering, Hugo walked between two trees and the circle of light cast by his torch increased, showing ... nothing. Curious, Arianna stepped into the clearing with Shade and looked around, but only darkness met her.

"We're here," Hugo yelled.

Her heartbeat sped up. Had Thales arranged to meet them here? Not wanting to wait for him to appear, Arianna cast a small white fire on her palm. It shone bright as if she had lit a hundred candles around them. It showed the small stones forming a circle in the center of the clearing, and delicate white flowers sprinkled here and there, their sweet fragrance filling the empty, dark space. She knew this place. It was a place of power, where she came to energize her magic every now and then. More important, it was close to the village.

Hugo had her walking in circles, and so welled in her

sorrow and letting the dark dictate her fear, she didn't pay attention.

Realizing this meant nothing good, the light flickered on her palm. Then it showed her five hooded men walking into the clearing from the other side.

Witch hunters from the Brotherhood.

Her heart jumped into her throat, and believing she would faint of fear, Arianna retreated. The light faded from her hand, and when she turned to run back into the woods, Hugo stepped in her way.

"Sorry, m'lady, but you're not going anywhere."

Goose bumps ran over her arms. "But Thales asked—"

"Prince Thales asked me to take you to safety, yes." He pointed his sword to her chest. "But the safest place for a witch is hell."

Before she could get through the confusion clouding her head, Hugo twisted the hilt of the sword in his hand and the pommel rushed to her face. She heard Shade whining as she fell into the darkness.

WHEN SHE OPENED HER EYES, ARIANNA GASPED, AWARE OF several things: complete darkness surrounded her; the moon was gone, hidden behind thick clouds. The right side of her face hurt and she was tied to a wooden post, her hands pulled tight behind it. Her necklace was gone and there were runes written on her arms and neck. With blood?

She jerked against the post, but that only made the rope bite into her skin and hurt her wrists.

Her mouth opened, ready to call for Hugo, but then she remembered the look of utter disgust on his face moments before he knocked her out. She glanced around the darkness. Where was he? Where were the witch hunters?

Tangible, the darkness pressed upon her, and she felt the chilly touch on her spine once more.

Arianna held her breath as the horde of ghosts circled her, forming a barrier of shrill and translucent bodies. Their expressions were grim and it broke her heart. She could feel them, their pain, their sadness, their desperate want for revenge.

Dear moon, what had she done?

The witch hunts were wiping Europe clean, and somehow the Brotherhood had found out about her existence. The existence of a powerful witch, the one that had founded the Lightgrove coven. Since then, the hunters went from town to town, looking for her, burning every young woman in their path.

If she had known the Brotherhood were so close to her village, she would have left, or hidden inside the palace. The king had promised to protect her after everything she did for his kingdom.

"Please," she whispered, fighting the panicked tears pressing behind her eyes. "I didn't mean to. I never meant for any of this to happen."

With the runes drawn on her skin, she could barely channel her power, let alone use her magic and send them away. Even if she were free and with her full magic, a passing ritual for so many would require a lot of ingredients and time, things she didn't have now.

The older women floated toward her, raising their decaying hands, exposing their razor-like teeth, their white dresses ripped and burned. They had died a couple of hours ago and already suffered through the in-between.

Arianna pressed her back to the post as if she could melt into it and disappear.

Half a dozen ghosts reached forward and their fingertips brushed against her. Pain shot through her veins from their touch and ran deep into her heart. It burned. It squeezed. It sped up.

She screamed.

But that only incited the ghosts to do more. They touched the runes drawn on her skin. Her head exploded, and pain swam inside her, in every single cell of her body. Black spots danced in the corners of her vision, and the world spun. She was losing it and she knew she would lose more than her consciousness.

"Help! Is somebody there?" With her blurry vision, she scanned the darkness, searching for anything, anyone. The ghosts wouldn't stay if someone else came. No, they wanted her and her alone. "Help!"

"Scream and call for help all you want," a hooded man said, emerging from the darkness.

The ghosts vanished and Arianna sagged against the post, putting her weight on the rope around her wrists. The pain hadn't left her yet, but it was diminishing. Slowly. Painfully.

She couldn't see his eyes under the heavy hood, only the small, evil grin on his lips as he lit a torch and taunted her with it, swaying the thing back and forth, closer and closer to her. Arianna straightened, trying to get away from it, pushing against the post.

"There's no one within five miles," Hugo said, coming into her line of sight. He wore the same cloak as the hunters, but his hood was down.

Arianna gaped at him. How was Thales fooled by this man?

The other four brothers appeared before her, the shadows cast by the torch dancing over their cloaks and hoods, making them almost as creepy as the ghosts.

"Let's start," one of them said.

Start what?

Panic replaced the pain inside her body, and Arianna jerked against the ropes again.

The torch was buried in the ground, and the five brothers knelt five feet from her, side-by-side, hands clasped together, and heads held low. They began praying.

Arianna knew those words. "I'm not like the other witches!" The tears were back to her eyes. "I'm not! I'm a light witch. A good witch. The king will vouch for me. Please."

"It doesn't matter," Hugo said. He unsheathed his sword. "No one should have any magic. It's the work of the Devil."

Putting on a brave face, she asked, "How did you fool Thales?"

"It was easy." Hugo pointed the sword to her throat.

She stifled a whimper. "I joined the Brotherhood after I was his trusted soldier." He leaned closer to her and whispered, his face only a few inches from her, "I was tired of the king and the prince preferring a witch to their own soldiers."

She opened her mouth to defend herself and Thales, but the tip of the sword pressed against her skin, and she closed her lips, elongating her neck as much as she could.

"Hugo, please," she said, her tone low and desperate. "You know I'm not evil. You know I can help bring down the evil witches. That's why I founded the Lightgrove coven."

He grazed the tip of the blade over her skin. "That also irks me. How can a nineteen-year-old accomplish so much?"

The voices of the brothers increased in volume and speed.

It was almost time.

A tear rolled down her cheek. "Please, Hugo."

Without a single ounce of remorse in his expressions, Hugo slid the blade from her throat to above her heart. "We can't allow you to roam this earth."

The brothers yelled their chant and Hugo's blade turned orange.

Arianna gasped as he drove it into her skin, only a quarter of an inch, but enough for the magic to work. Blood trickled down her dress and the orange shine floated from the blade into her wound. When all of it was inside her, he withdrew his sword and retreated, his eyes wide.

For her, they had saved their special weapon, a *magical* weapon—to be burned from the inside.

Arianna screamed as the spell spread through her chest like spiderwebs, burning every inch of her body. She couldn't think through the pain. Only feel. Feel her organs dying, her heart slowing, her breathing failing.

Looking down, she saw her skin graying. Shade lay at her feet, meowing sadly as if he could help her with his voice.

Arianna closed her eyes and gritted her teeth.

This is it. My end.

If only she could see Thales one las—

"Arianna!" Thales voice echoed through the clearing, and she opened her eyes.

There he was, her prince, beautifully clad in his leather armor, his sword in his hand, brandishing it against the Brothers and Hugo. There was something fierce on his handsome face as he and his soldiers killed the men who had doomed her, a glint of pure rage and desperation in his beautiful blue eyes. Goddess, why had she resisted his advances for over six months? He was a prince, yes, but he was *her* prince.

The torch was knocked over and doused, leaving them in almost complete darkness. She could see and feel the ghosts around the clearing, waiting for her. But for now, she ignored them.

Arianna smiled as Thales rushed to her. He cut her ropes and held her in his arms before her body slid to the ground.

It hurt. All of it. The burning inside her, and the knowledge that she was dying. The knowledge that she would be permanently separated from Thales. And it wouldn't be for what they had feared. Not by politics or royalty, but by death.

"My love," he whispered, his words thick with his pain. He held her tight against his chest. This couldn't be happening. "I'm so sorry. I had no idea."

"Shhh." Arianna raised a gray hand and caressed his cheek, her fingers rough from the spell within her. Swallowing a sob, Thales held the hand to his face. "It's okay. You're here now."

Her voice was cracking, just like the rest of her body. It was a terrible vision, the way her body grayed and burned from the inside out.

"What can I do? Tell me. Any magic, any spells, I'll do it." He reached for her neck. "Where's your necklace?"

"They took it," she said, her voice fainter and fainter.

"Please, Arianna." A sob ripped through his throat. "There must be something we can do."

But there wasn't. He could see it in her glassy eyes and her almost dead body. His heart was dying too.

With one hand, he took out his cloak and spread it beside him. Gently, he deposited her over it, lying beside her, keeping her close to him.

Gods, what had he done to deserve this? She was the most perfect creature in the whole world. Why let her die?

Arianna choked and her body quavered, the fire inside

it surging up under the gray skin. "Remember … that I love you."

He looked into her eyes, her bright green eyes, and fought the tears wanting to assault him. "And I love you." He leaned down and kissed her lips. "We'll be together again. I promise," he whispered in her ear.

With a loud gasp, Arianna's body went slack in his arms. The fire shone through and ashes fell over his cloak.

Thales knelt and brought his head to the ground. He screamed. In rage. In sorrow. In desperation. In love. He had found the one and only for him, and had lost her.

It was his fault too, letting her alone with one of his soldiers. He should have been the one to take her out of town and to safety.

After a long time of mourning and cursing, Thales gathered his cloak into a makeshift sack, careful to keep Arianna's ashes inside.

He stood with the sack secured in his hands, and raised it to the sky, asking for the blessing of the darkness. "I'll bring you back, my love. Somehow, I'll find a way to bring you back."

With Shade by his side, Thales turned his back to the post and walked into the woods, welcoming the numbing darkness.

who finds out she's a demon hunter, and the half-demon intent on protecting her against all evil.

The Vampire Heir (Rite World 1: Rite of the Vampire): a dark and mysterious paranormal romance about a vampire and a young woman with a secret.

The Warlock Lord (Rite World 4: Rite of the Warlock): a thrilling and kick-ass paranormal romance about a were-wolf and warlock.

The Wolf Forsaken (Rite World 7: Rite of the Wolf): a heat-wrenching tale about a lost wolf shifter and a fae princess on the run.

Heart Seeker (The Fire Heart Chronicles book 1): an urban fantasy series about a young woman who finds herself at the center of a mysterious supernatural world.

Destiny Gift (The Everlast Series book 1): a post-apocalyptic urban fantasy series about a young woman with a special power that can save the world.

DON'T FORGET TO SIGN UP FOR MY NEWSLETTER TO FIND OUT about new releases, cover reveals, giveaways, and more!

If you want to see exclusive teasers, help me decide on covers, read excerpts, talk about books, etc, join my reader group on Facebook: Juliana's Club!

EXTEND YOUR STAY IN THE RITE WORLD

WHICH FREE BOOK WILL YOU CHOOSE NEXT?

The Vampire Heir

The Demon Kiss

Continue swiping to know more …

MEET DRAKE AND THEA

The Vampire Heir

A YOUNG WOMAN WITH A SECRET. A VAMPIRE WITH A DEATH *sentence. And a terrible fate that will destroy them both...*

Thea

When I was invited to Castle DuMoir, I knew I'd end up dead. The guests might be excited by the exclusive ball inside the estate, but I know better. The castle's inhabitants are vampires, and they want our blood.

Undercover work is dangerous, but I've been through worse. That is, until I unwillingly become a blood slave to Drake, the brooding vampire prince.

Desire begins to stir, but I can't afford distractions. My dark secret will save us all... or doom the supernatural world forever.

Drake

I didn't think love existed. Then I met Thea.

Vampires aren't supposed to have a heart. But mine beats for her. Yet I can't protect Thea in a castle full of conspiracies and betrayal. The vampires are about to choose the coven's new leader, and there's a murderer running loose.

After everything I've done, I thought that I was the most dangerous monster in existence. I'm not even close.

MEET ERIN AND REY

The Demon Kiss

A YOUNG WOMAN WITH A SECRET HERITAGE. A MAN WHO MADE a deal with the devil. And an academy where the students are just as dangerous as the demons ...

Erin

I've been kept from the truth all my life. Demons walk the earth, and I'm destined to slay them--I only wish I hadn't lost someone I loved while discovering that truth.

Now the demons are after me. The only way to stay alive is to attend an academy for demon hunters--a school where I'll learn how to kill supernaturals and slay the underworld's minions. But I still feel there are secrets I'm not being told ...

Rey

I sold my soul to save my family--and lost everything because of it. Now I'm a slave to the underworld, a fake hunter with half-demon blood.

I've been sent on a special assassination mission. If I fail, it means my life. But protecting Erin soon becomes more important than any other task, and there's something about her that tells me her arrival at the academy will change everything ...

ABOUT THE AUTHOR

While USA Today Bestselling Author Juliana Haygert dreams of being Wonder Woman, Buffy, or a blood elf shadow priest, she settles for the less exciting—but equally gratifying—life as a wife, a mother, and an author. She resides in North Carolina and spends her days writing about kick-ass heroines and the heroes who drive them crazy.

Subscribe to her mailing list to receive emails of announcement, events, and other fun stuff related to her writing and her books: www.bit.ly/JuHNL

For more information:
www.julianahaygert.com

facebook.com/julianahaygert

twitter.com/julianahaygert

instagram.com/juliana.haygert

goodreads.com/juliana_haygert

pinterest.com/julianahaygert

bookbub.com/authors/juliana-haygert

youtube.com/julianahaygert

tiktok.com/@julianahaygert

ALSO BY JULIANA HAYGERT

To find links and more info, go to:
www.julianahaygert.com/books/

Shorts
Into the Darkest Fire

Standalones
Daughter of Darkness

Rite World: Night Wolves
The Night Calling (Book 1)
The Night Burning (Book 2)
The Night Hunting (Book 3)
The Night Rising (Book 4)

Rite World: Vampire Wars
The Darkest Vampire (Book 1)
The Darkest Witch (Book 2)
The Darkest Magic (Book 3)

Rite World: Lightgrove Witches
The Midnight Test (Book 1)
The Midnight Spell (Book 2)
The Midnight Flame (Book 3)
The Midnight Secret (Book 4)

Rite World: Blackthorn Hunters Academy
The Demon Kiss (Book 1)
The Hunter Secret (Book 2)
The Soul Bond (Book 3)

The Shadow Trials (Book 4)
The Infernal Curse (Book 5)

<u>Rite World</u>
The Vampire Heir (Book 1)
The Witch Queen (Book 2)
The Immortal Vow (Book 3)
The Warlock Lord (Book 4)
The Wolf Consort (Book 5)
The Crystal Rose (Book 6)
The Wolf Forsaken (Book 7)
The Fae Bound (Book 8)
The Blood Pact (Book 9)

The Wyth Courts
Winter King (Book 1)
Spring Warrior (Book 2)
Summer Prince (Book 3)
Autumn Rebel (Book 4)

The Fire Heart Chronicles
Heart Seeker (Book 1)
Flame Caster (Book 2)
Earth Shaker (Book 2.5)
Sorrow Bringer (Book 3)
Soul Wanderer (Book 4)
Fate Summoner (Book 5)
War Maiden (Book 6)

The Everlast Series
Destiny Gift (Book 1)
Soul Oath (Book 2)
Cup of Life (Book 3)
Everlasting Circle (Book 4)

Willow Harbor Series
Hunter's Revenge (Book 3)

Siren's Song (Book 5)

Breaking Series
Breaking Free (Book 1)
Breaking Away (Book 2)
Breaking Through (Book 3)
Breaking Down (Book 4)